Threats and Challenges

Also by Jerry Labriola

—Murders at Hollings General

—Murders at Brent Institute

—The Maltese Murders

—The Strange Death of Napoleon Bonaparte

—Scent of Danger

—Object of Betrayal

—Deadly Politics

—Global Shadows

—Diamonds and Pirates

—Dangerous Triangle

—The Blue Baron Mystery

—The Saga of Hodge

—Spying for Keeps

—Discovery

—On the Right Track

Coauthored with Dr. Henry Lee

—Famous Crimes Revisited

—Forensic Files

—The Budapest Connection

—Shocking Cases

Threats and Challenges

A NOVEL

By

JERRY LABRIOLA, M.D.

STRONG BOOKS

Strong Books
P.O. Box 715
Avon, CT 06001-0715

First Printing

ISBN 978-1-928782-71-1

Library of Congress Control Number: 2020934370

Published in the United States of America by Strong Books, an imprint of Publishing Directions, LLC

Printed in the United States of America

Dedicated to Grady,
Xavier's newly born brother
— another joy

ACKNOWLEDGMENTS

My sincere thanks to all the personnel at STRONG BOOKS

NOTE

— To avoid the complexities of different languages spoken, all are delivered in English.

— Names of the main characters are figments of my imagination.

— Since there are numerous meetings among characters, all formal introductions and handshakes have been minimized in number.

— Some parts of this book contain paragraphs taken from other books I have written.

— Details of getting from one place to another are not always given.

PREFACE

The following sources have been most helpful. Some descriptive materials have been taken from them — with minor modifications. Much credit is due their authors. Apologies are extended for the accidental omission of some sources.

BBC Reports
INTERPOL
Looted Art
Central European Waterways
ABA Journal
The Lee/Labriola Books
Wall Street Journal
Travel Planner
From PlanetWare
Travel and Leisure
Search for Missing Art
French Connection
Paris
Lonely Planet Review
Peter's Paris
French Academy of Sciences
Les Invalides
Terrorism
Notre-Dame of Paris
Eiffel Tower
Champs Élysées
Nazi Plunder
Pilgrim Monument

New York Times Encyclopedia Britannica
The 20th Century
The Secret History of World War II
The World of Spies
The British World
The National World War ll Museum
Biography of Juan Peron
History of Switzerland
Sicilian Mafia
Vichy, France
Cordoba, Argentina
Switzerland During the World Wars
Wikipedia

PART ONE

Threats and Challenges
Chapter 1

Early March, 2006

Criminal investigator and former security consultant for nearby Hollings Hospital, Rick Chandler couldn't believe he might be cutting short his vacation. It was the result of a phone call from Leon Cassell, the chairman of *Gens de Vérité*, an ancient French organization noted for protecting the national security of countries that sought its help. The two men had worked together so many times over the years that Leon had finally decided to rent an apartment not far from Rick's home in Connecticut.

"Rick? I have good news for you."

"Good news? You just made it worse by calling me."

"No really, you won't believe this. I just received a call from a Hollywood movie mogul. He wants to produce a movie about … wait … are you sitting?"

"On the edge of my bed. You just woke me. It's not even eight in the morning here."

"Sorry about that but this will get you going. He wants the movie to be about a real-life Dracula taking on the so-called 'Butcher of the Balkans', Slobodan Milosevic. He was a Yugoslavian and Serbian politician, eventual president of both countries, and was arrested in early 2001 on suspicion of corruption, abuse of power and embezzlement. This didn't stand though, so he was arrested instead on charges of war crimes.

"But the mogul wants to have the story in book form … I mean he wants to have a book written about it, and then he'll make his own script from it. He's used to producing movies that way. I asked how come, and he dodged the question."

The idea of a movie struck a chord. When Rick was a high school senior, he had tried out for a role in a Hollywood movie. The producer said he liked the performance … "but we'd have to cut your fluffy hair."

Rick refused.

"Why not?" the producer asked.

"Because I have some white hairs that my fluff hides."

"So we'll cut those, too."

"No. Then I'd be bald."

"Let's forget it and thanks for coming here. Okay?"

"Okay."

Rick was only slightly sorry he'd made the cross-country trip and, for the first time, he'd learned never to get his hopes up so easily. In addition, he thought that as long as he was where big-time movies were made, he would look around, ask questions of people who appeared to be important there, and generally make the journey one that might serve him well in the future.

"Hello," Leon said. "Can you still hear me?"

"I suppose so."

"Bottom line then," Leon continued, "would you be interested in writing that kind of book?"

Rick scratched his head and said, "Christ, normally I'd say 'no', though the Dracula thing is tempting. For now, let's say maybe. But how's this related to national security?"

"It's stretching a point, I guess, but when we hear 'Milosevic', we think of Balkan countries, like Serbia, and Croatia and Bosnia-Herzegovina. And I'm not sure if Kosovo's a country yet, but even there."

"Hmm … all places I intend to visit someday. But tell me about Dracula. Isn't he imaginary?"

"Yes and no. For our purposes, he'd be real. Sometimes."

"So he's sometimes real and sometimes not." It was a statement, not a question.

"It's up to you, Rick. Handle it as you see fit. One thing's for certain, though: the producer said his company has heard of you, and if the movie comes to pass it's willing to pay you 25% of all royalties."

"No, no, my friend. You know how that works. I'm well-healed and the money should go to Vérité."

Rick's facial expression reflected that he'd already reached a positive decision. "Would I highlight anything?" he asked.

"No, just write as if you'd planned on it anyway. I even have a title for you: *Dracula's Revenge*. Or if not that, maybe *Dracula Becomes Real*. You might start the book by writing about a visit to some of the countries but, to begin with, you stop by Transylvania and Dracula's Castle."

"And in the book, I'm myself and I spend time in some Balkan countries?"

"That's it. You're in the countries during the day and you write about it in the evening."

"But why? I mean why would I be going there in the first place?"

"You'd have to figure it out, but offhand you might have been asked to work with local police in avoiding a clash between Dracula and Milosevic. Somehow you've heard of that as a possibility. And whether or not the dictator is guilty of war crimes could be treated as second fiddle to the Dracula/Milosevic issue."

"But getting back to that producer … how do we know he's legit?" Rick continued as he made notes in a pad he'd taken from a nightstand drawer.

"I already checked on him, and he's very legit."

Most of the conversation ended with Rick now fully awake and ready to tackle another challenge. He loved challenges that didn't somehow drain his ego however. Like that one in Hollywood … years before. He had almost been cast for a certain movie because of his appearance (he was told): a solid six feet tall and muscular, with light blue eyes and a square jaw. But when the producer and director heard of his age … thirty-five at the time … he was cast aside.

He looked the same today except he was two to three inches taller, graying and longer hair and more piercing brown eyes.

After a brief lull, Leon's "thank you" sounded fueled with a burst of energy. And seconds prior to that, Rick had said that he'd begin writing the book the next evening. During the morning though, they would first land in Bucharest and then drive to Transylvania. Next would come the beginning of visits to a few of the Balkan countries. Rick asked Leon to arrange for a flight beginning at one a.m. to allow for the time zone difference. In turn, Vérité's chairman repeated what he had said a minute earlier: "Visit countries during the day and write about them at night, and I'll be glad to go with you."

Leon's *Gens de Vérité* had been in existence for more than two centuries. It was a private group that worked alongside the government and was noted for solving many worldwide puzzles. It was in this connection that Leon had regularly sought Rick's assistance. The chairman had a strong connection with the Royal Air Force out of London and with one of its arms, the Joint Base Cape Cod … JBCC … located in Hyannis, not far from Rick's home and Leon's apartment in Connecticut. One of JBCC's smaller planes manned by a pilot friend, Ansel Stewart, would usually remain at designated locations, awaiting further instructions from Rick. Airport personnel would even dispatch a limo to and from his home whenever it was needed. And he was allowed to be armed with a shoulder and ankle gun on every flight, as was Leon.

Rick and his wife, Angela, lived in New Haven, not far from the Yale Bowl. He'd graduated from Yale where he majored in languages, notably Spanish, French and German. He was often called upon to investigate crimes or working security at Hollings General. It was located in Hollings, a small manufacturing town ten miles north of New Haven. And he was busy learning more and more about forensic science from Dr. Henry Lee at Quinnipiac University. There, he also mastered karate, having earned black belt status 15-years earlier. It hadn't taken long for him to gain atemiwaza expertise whereby he could kick an adversary and cause paralysis or even death. So with such karate moves and constantly armed with his two guns … a Beretta Cougar .45 in a shoulder holster and a Heritage Stealth 9 mm in an ankle rig, he was confident he'd come out a winner in any personal attack.

Later, the black belt status led to a position at Bruno's Martial Arts Studio where he taught a beginner's class on most Thursday mornings. Its director understood Rick's unpredictable schedule and allowed him to miss some of the sessions. The director himself would then fill in.

The only other thing that was constantly at his side was a bulging satchel. Overly stuffed with technical equipment and other things he'd collected over the years, it was as wide as it was deep. Also in it were papers he would never leave behind, especially the ones dealing with talks he'd given on a variety of topics over the years.

As for the Chandler house, it had a steeply pitched, hipped roof and single story facades that were asymmetrical. Its doors and windows were arched upward, extending through the cornice line. Outside there was little to a front lawn, but in a deep back side there were thick green shrubs and clusters of black-eyed Susans, Shasta daisies and other perennials. They were all arranged in geometric patterns. And through it all was a winding flagstone path of bricks with moss that separated them. He paid Yale students to maintain the whole area.

Inside, there were nine rooms, all on one floor. The largest was a master bedroom and surrounding it were three guest bedrooms. The kitchen was narrow but long as were a dining room, living room and family room. And there were bathrooms at every turn. Angela often expressed pride about her having brightened the living room by displaying some hanging wicker and rope accents along with faux flowers on a coffee table.

Rick's study was large but plain and square and had been fixed up as an office: computer, printer, copier, fax machine, two phones, file cabinets, surrounding shelves stacked with books, and two desks … one a sit-down, one a stand-up.

He often walked through a laundry room, breezeway and two-car garage into what he called his "meditation grounds" where he would wander around, never consulting his wristwatch. Once settled on a wooden bench, he would listen hard for sounds of the not-too-distant forest, like wind through its trees.

But it was three other undertakings that occupied any of Rick's non-investigative time. The first two were writing and sightseeing. He was currently on his sixth forensic science book and the sightseeing would be squeezed into any worldwide investigations. As a longtime admirer of Napoleon, another book he wrote was about him. He wrote it several years ago, titled it *The Strange Death of Napoleon Bonaparte* and kept it in his satchel. And the third was the aforementioned martial arts class.

As for Angela, she was as busy as her husband. A psychologist and Harvard graduate, she was on the Board of Directors of the American Psychological Association and worked full time overseeing the affairs of its graduate students. For most days of the week, full time translated into overtime and, as a result, she was unable to accompany Rick on any of his travels.

She was the first person he called … to inform her of his decision. He could have done so later that evening but by now, he was too hepped up to wait. Her response was the usual one. If one were listening in, her initial words would have sounded cold and distant, but he knew better. "What else is new?" she asked. "Just be sure to call me on a regular basis. And be careful. Maybe your most dangerous mission. I'll be praying."

"I will too, Ange. For both of us."

Next, he phoned his good friend, Fran Moreau who, he hoped, would accompany him as usual. Fran agreed.

Then once again he knew that, sooner or later, he'd be consulting with some other longtime colleagues. He made calls asking for support, if needed, over the foreseeable few days.

To Buenos Aires police chief, Joseph Gomez, requesting him to alert fellow chiefs in the capitals of all the Balkan countries that he would be visiting. And indicating that he — Rick — is accustomed to giving free talks on numerous subjects such as terrorism, mythology, and the new genetics. Rick mentioned that auditorium talks often encouraged the chiefs to help out as best they could. "But don't ever tell them what I have in mind. I'll do that myself."

To Paul D'Arneau, a criminalist whose advice was always viewed as vital to Rick.

To Fabio Calderone who once lived in Calabria, Italy but had since moved to Chicago. He was a former commander of the Padrino, the second highest level of the 'Ndrangrata organization within the entire Mafia. He had given it all up, however, claiming weariness and a desire to be "more legal and more American" after attending various schools in the Chicago area. Through several years, he and Rick had formed a firm bond.

And to Lance Beck, the regional leader of a group of men and women who went by the name of histarians — not historians. Not an "o" but an "a". Numbering 2,000 world-wide members, they would provide information on any topic that might be brought up by Lance — all done in tight secrecy. Rick, in fact, had sought their help before … through Leon

— and had received totally correct information. Toward the end of the call, Rick said to Lance:

"Tell me something. Where do they get their information?"

"Nobody knows, but it's 100% accurate. They say that if what they find out is questionable, they don't offer it."

"Not even a suggestion?"

"Not even a suggestion."

The answer from each of the four men was a resounding yes. And Leon had added that he'd notify Ansel Stewart, the skilled and always available pilot and driver. He would also notify Lance about having his histarian 'brigade' ready to monitor the whereabouts of Dracula each and every day.

Also, Gomez had said he'd supply Rick with a list of all the Balkan chiefs in the capital cities he'd contacted. Which, at the time, reminded Rick that he'd better advise his colleagues of the order of his visits. "Unless, of course, we run into pal Dracula and put a stop to his plans."

Later that evening, Rick received a call from Gomez who gave the names of the first four chiefs he had contacted. He indicated that they would be happy to welcome him and would introduce him to as large an audience as they could muster up. Rick wrote the names of the capital cities and their police chiefs in his pad:

—Belgrade, Serbia. Karl Hinter

—Budapest, Hungary. Fritz Elser

—Zugreb, Croatia. Jan Funck

—Ljubljana, Slovenia. Nikolas Shultz

Before calling it a night, he downloaded a computer article about Transylvania and Count Dracula. He read it carefully:

Transylvania is a mountainous region in the center of Bucharest, the capital of Romania. The Carpathian Mountains and Transylvanian Alps separate the region from the rest of Romania. Romanians and Hungarians often quarreled over Transylvania. During World War I, Romania joined the Allies after being promised Transylvania. After the war, Transylvania became part of Romania. However, in 1940, Germany and Italy forced Romania to give northern Transylvania to Hungary. Then, after World War II, Transylvania was returned to Romania and lost its political identity.

Transylvania is the main site of the legend about the famous vampire, Dracula. The character is based on Vlad Tepes, a cruel prince of the 1400's. He executed many of his enemies by driving a sharpened pole through their bodies. A belief in vampires formerly held by many Romanian peasants added details to the legend. Dracula, a novel by the English author Bram Stoker, made the legend internationally famous.

This immensely popular book has inspired numerous plays and movies.

Chapter 2

The first destination was Bucharest, Romania. Fran, Leon and Ansel accompanied Rick as they landed at the Otopeni Airport.

Rick was always taken with how physically dissimilar the men looked. Fran, the tallest, had wavy dark hair, a wiry mustache and a right forearm that bore a small tattoo of the American flag. Leon, of average height, was paunchy, nearly bald, and offered a handshake that nearly brought greeters to their knees. And Ansel … short, thin, blond hair, blue eyes, inconspicuous. But their clothing always matched: blue blazer, tie, black loafers.

Ansel rented a car and it took only two hours to drive into Transylvania. It was a mountainous region in the center of the country and a slight mist had turned into a pelting rain as they passed through the treacherous Carpathian Mountain Pass. They had expected some snow but instead, a late morning humidity tasted and smelled like no other.

Fran and Leon were seated in the back of the car, a very small Dacia, while Rick's six-foot-three frame barely fit into the passenger seat. He had insisted on that location, however, for it would then be easier to take pictures of the medieval villages and fortified churches that they encountered. And all the while, he had no idea if they might be catching up to a real-life Dracula.

Is this all a joke?

It was not hard for them to spot *Dracula's Castle* up on a mountain top. As they studied it from below, it appeared spread out in grey sections that were crowned with orange triangular tops. Rick assumed that the tops were meant to attract attention.

Ansel pulled the Dacia into a parking lot filled with tour buses, and they piled out. They then followed a mob of tourists up a long ramp and countless steps to its entrance. Once inside, there were more steps leading to a dark narrow corridor. All the footsteps echoed as if trying to gain control. They lagged so far behind and Rick felt so hungry that he suggested they turn around, go for lunch and then return.

"I think that when we do return, we should walk faster than now and even excuse ourselves as we force our way through the line. We might even say we have an appointment inside."

The Dracula Restaurant was within walking distance of the castle. It had no signs, just a panel that opened speakeasy style. It looked more like a luxury house than an eating place. Out front was a stone façade with bay windows. Inside there was sunny wallpaper with period silhouettes. Chairs were carved to resemble Indian palaces; dollhouses were scattered around; and gossamer-winged chandeliers topped the scene.

They gave their names, were allowed in and were directed along a hallway to the "hunt room". It had dark wood wainscoting, a pitched ceiling, and animal skins dangling in all corners.

After an indifferent meal served by an indifferent waitress, the lights became dim, and deep organ music nearly drowned out a woman's distant screams. Suddenly a door creaked open and a supposed Dracula appeared carrying a candelabra with dripping red candles. Tall and cadaverous, he wore a dark tuxedo, dark bow-tie and a black cape lined in red. A stiff white collar rose up as a triangle in front. Matted down grey hair ran around a head that was way too large for his body and lateral incisor teeth hung down over his lower lip. His complexion was drained of color.

"Goood e-ven-ing," he said, sucking back a spot supposed supposed of blood. "I would have joined you, but I have already dined." There was a red light of triumph in his green eyes and he was slow in fashioning a smile that Judas in hell might have been proud of. His comment over, he swirled around and drifted away.

Rick wondered why evening had been mentioned when it was barely noontime.

He then signaled for the waitress, saying he had some questions about what just transpired.

"Sorry," she said. "I only work here and I'm not allowed to talk about Dracula. You'd have to check over at the castle."

They returned to the hunt room and did just what Rick had suggested before. Once ahead of the mob and past hidden passageways, they began walking on an enormous bear rug sprawled across the floor. He looked out a window and saw a small black Dacia drive up and a short man getting out of it. Once in the room, he approached them and said, "My name is Alex Prisco, the manager here. May I help you?"

"Yes indeed," Rick said. " May I ask you some questions?"

"Of course. Let us go in here." He led them into a small room, closed the door, and locked it.

Rick stared at the man and, for the first time in months, he was ready to unleash a karate chop, but it wasn't needed.

Alex unlocked the door after noticing their expressions.

"Good," Rick said. "First off, do you see much of your Dracula? And if so, do you talk?"

"No, not much. Only if he is going away for something. So he tells me."

"You mean where he's going?"

"Yes. He will not leave notes. He has to **tell** me. It is never at night though, because he is too busy lying on his back and staring at the ceiling." Alex was enunciating his words clearly.

"He doesn't sleep?" Rick asked.

"He calls that sleeping. But his eyes are open and staring."

"Understood. And maybe our most important question. It's really why we're here in the first place. We hear that he is after Slobodan Milosevic. Why is that?"

"Because he says he has heard that the man is responsible for many, many deaths and he wants to bite him and turn him into a vampire. Our Dracula can control vampires. That is what he says."

"Is he real?"

"Real? Yes. All the time? I do not know. I inquired once and, in return, he asked if I wanted to become a vampire."

"And where is he now?"

"I think somewhere in the rest of Romania."

"But why is there a Dracula living here in the first place?"

"Because he is the draw for people who then flock here for souvenirs."

"Like what?"

"Like little statues of him; or postcards of Balkan cities; or pens and pencils; or many other things like scarfs or gloves or toys for kids. I remember very well the time I spent in your Brooklyn selling these kinds of things. They are downstairs in a special room. Do you wish to buy any of what we have to offer?"

"No, not today. But you spent time in Brooklyn?"

"Born there and moved here five years ago. I interviewed for this position and I was hired."

Rick then asked the other three if they had questions. In doing so, he noticed that they looked spellbound, even Leon. But it was Fran who finally responded: "I think we're behind in our schedule, so we'd better leave."

They thanked Alex and then Fran said to him, “Now if you become a vampire, do still recognize us, okay? Which reminds me: Do vampires talk?”

“Yes, they do talk but they are hard to understand. Not for Dracula, however. He and his vampires understand everybody. Even when everybody is nobody.”

Nothing is straightforward lately.

Before leaving Transylvania, Rick phoned Gomez, Lance and Paul to give them the order of the upcoming visits. “We won’t do more here in Romania,” he said, “but tomorrow we begin in Serbia, then on to Hungary, and maybe Croatia to start with. He also indicated the titles of his first three talks: “Terrorism”; “The Myth of Mythology“; and “DNA and the New Genetics”.

They began a drive to nearby Brasov, one of the seven citadel cities established by Teutonic knights in the 13th century. Rick had once read about what they soon saw: striking houses with ornate carving, pastel-washed facades and windows flanked by wood shutters. The dwellings stood out like orchids in a field of more practically built Romanian-style homes encircling the wide Brasov Square. They passed the famous Gothic Black Church where a life-size statue of a man slouched eerily above its entrance. Glistening glass eyes were inserted in sockets and streaky long hair was plastered on the man’s head. Rick shivered as he thought the slouch, the eyes and the hair resembled his own.

Just beyond the church, they saw horse-driven wagons and fields dotted with haystack domes and sheep tended by shepherds on cellphones.

“Cellphones and sheep … new times added to old times,” Rick said.

They turned back to a motel near the Square and called it a day. He had decided not to begin writing about the day’s activities, yet would do so before retiring the following night. But when asleep, a dream focused on each of the activities.

During breakfast there in the morning, Rick said, "Fair warning to you guys. I'm sure there'll be informative posters at each airport we reach … about the city and whatever. Join me if you wish, but I'm reading all of them."

That had been his habit. He not only read such posters but often took pictures of them for future reference, inserting them into his overstuffed satchel. Sometimes when he felt short of arm strength, he would alternate hands in handling it, vowing that one day he would buy a shoulder strap.

Chapter 3

After landing back at the Otopenia Airport and before taking the one-hour commercial flight to the Nicola Tesla Airport in Serbia's capital city, Rick received another call from Gomez. The number of calls he'd been receiving was double the number he received while at home … while he was just writing.

Gomez indicated that Chief Karl Hassel's office was in the center of the city and that he had arranged for the students of two high schools to be gathered at one of their assembly halls. They'd be awaiting Rick's talk at eleven a.m. The Serbian chief then gave directions to his office building, saying that they should first discuss why there had to be Balkan meetings in general and there in Serbia specifically.

At the airport, Rick looked for and found a poster about the country and while the others waited, he read through it:

> Serbia is a country situated at the crossroads of Central and southeast Europe in the southern Pannonian Plain and the central Balkans. It borders Hungary to the north, Romania to the northeast, Bulgaria to the southeast, North Macedonia to the south, Croatia and Bosnia-Herzegovina to the west, and Montenegro to the southwest. The country claims a border with Albania through the disputed territory of Kosovo. Serbia's population numbers approximately seven million, most of whom are Orthodox Christians. Its capital, Belgrade, ranks among the longest inhabited and largest cities in southeastern Europe.
>
> In the early 19th century, the Serbian Revolution established the nation-state as the region's first constitutional monarchy, which

> subsequently expanded its territory. Following disastrous casualties in World War 1, and the subsequent unification of other territories with Serbia, the country co-founded Yugoslavia with other South Slavic peoples, which would exist in various political formations until the Yugoslav Wars of the 1990s. During the breakup of Yugoslavia, Serbia formed a union with Montenegro which was peacefully dissolved this year.

There! The first one to be read, and I did it!

They took a cab to the office building which Rick scanned before they entered. He couldn't believe it but instead of observing a pale hue, he thought what was before them wouldn't look out of place in the catalog of a furniture retailer that prided itself over a restrained purple background.

They were greeted cordially and sat in a wide circle of chairs with the chief at its center. The chairs of the quartet were straight backed while the chief's was a swivel. One would hardly miss the nature of his calling: pressed blue uniform brimming with gold and silver badges; service stripes along both arms; epaulets on both shoulders.

Rick wasted no time in explaining what would probably be a two-week-long mission. "It's a case of Dracula versus Milosevic," he said, "and we're prepared to assist in preventing bloodshed, whether from the vampire's mouth or the dictator's head. So please call me if you become suspicious of either of these taking place here in Serbia. We can then help radio surrounding areas that you feel should be notified. And If, by chance, Milosevic happens to call on you and he hasn't heard about Dracula's intention, do tell him about it and ask him to lay low as much as he can. I don't think staying in one place is best. He should be traveling around instead, but always secretly. *Semper paratus* ...'always ready'. It's the motto of our U.S. Coast Guard."

The chief tilted his head, listening as if he were detecting the sounds of a distant coyote. He finally spoke.

"You believe in a Dracula?"

"Yes and no. Some days I do, some I don't."

"But because it's all so serious … so deadly I should say … we should be paratus?"

"Yes, and one last thing, chief. My talk will be about terrorism and I'll read directly from a book I wrote. It deals with forensic science. But if it's alright with you, I won't take questions for we're on a tight schedule. The same kind of discussion we just had will take place in some other Balkan countries. Hope you understand."

"I certainly do and I wish you all the luck in the world or at least here in the Balkans. And also with your talk."

At roughly ten-forty, Hassel led the drive to the Belgrade High School and, ten minutes later, all five men entered the assembly hall. It was filled to capacity with students and faculty members. All cheered and some of the students were waving small American flags.

The chief pointed to three chairs on a corner of the stage and Fran, Leon and Ansel climbed up to sit on them. He then preceded Rick to the podium and gave a brief introduction which included a request that no questions should be asked after the talk. "Our congenial guests have a full schedule for the day and we should honor that," he said.

Amidst loud clapping, Rick took out a book from his overstuffed satchel and flipped to a page marked with a folded sheet of paper. He then began:

"Thank you, one and all. You may have heard that I'll be reading the pages from a book I wrote some years ago. The subject will be 'Terrorism' and the reason I've chosen it is because some of you may study to become a forensic scientist, and those of you who do will certainly deal with such a subject. So let's get on with it … and do take notes if you wish.

"Terrorism is, in the broadest sense, the use of indiscriminate violence as a means to create terror among masses of people; or fear to achieve a religious or political aim. It is used in this regard primarily to refer to violence during peacetime or in the context of war against non-combatants … mostly civilians and neutral military personnel. The terms 'terrorist' and 'terrorism' originated during the French Revolution of the late 18th century but gained mainstream popularity in the 1970s in news reports and books covering the conflicts in Northern Ireland, the Basque Country and Palestine. The increased use of suicide attacks from the 1980s onward was typified by the September 11 attacks in New York City and Washington, D.C. in 2001.

There are different definitions of terrorism. It's a charged term. It is often used with the connotation of something that is 'morally wrong'. Governments and non-state groups use the term to abuse or denounce opposing groups. Varied political organizations have been accused of using terrorism to achieve their objectives. These organizations include right-wing and left-wing political organizations, nationalist groups, religious groups, revolutionaries and ruling governments. Legislation declaring terrorism a crime has been adopted in many states. When terrorism is perpetrated by nation-states, it is not considered terrorism by the state perpetrating it, making legality a largely grey-area issue. There is no consensus as to whether or not terrorism should be considered a war crime.

There are over 109 different definitions of terrorism. American political philosopher Michael in 2002 wrote: 'Terrorism is the deliberate killing of innocent people, at random, to spread fear through a whole population and force the hand of its political leaders.'

Experts disagree about whether terrorism is wrong by definition or just wrong as a matter of fact; they disagree about whether it should be defined in terms of its aims, or its methods, or both, or neither; they even disagree about whether or not states can perpetrate terrorism.

In November 2004, a Secretary-General of the United Nations described terrorism as any act 'intended to cause death or serious bodily harm to civilians or non-combatants with the purpose of intimidating a population or compelling a government or an international organization to do or abstain from doing any act.' The international community has been slow to formulate a universally agreed upon, legally binding definition of this crime. These difficulties arise from the fact that the term 'terrorism' is politically and emotionally charged.

A brief to the Australian parliament stated, 'The international community has never succeeded in developing an accepted comprehensive definition of terrorism. During the 1970s and 1980s, the United Nations' attempts to define the term floundered, mainly due to differences of opinion between various members about the use of violence in the context of conflicts over national liberation and self-liberation.'

Since 1994, the United States General Assembly has repeatedly condemned terrorist attacks, using the following political description of terrorism: 'Criminal acts' intended or calculated to provoke a state of terror in the public, or to a group of persons for political purposes.

'International terrorism' means activities with the following three characteristics: One … Involve violent acts or acts dangerous to human life that violate federal or state law. Two … Appear to be intended to intimidate or coerce a civilian population; to influence the policy of a government by intimidation or coercion; or to affect the conduct of a government by mass destruction, assassination, or kidnapping. And Three … Occur primarily outside the territorial jurisdiction of the U.S., or transcend national boundaries in terms of the means by which they are accomplished, the persons they appear intended to intimidate or coerce, or the locale in which their perpetrators operate or seek asylum.

Since 9/11, there has been a five-fold increase in deaths from terrorist attacks. The majority of incidents over the past several years can be tied to groups with a religious agenda. Before 2000, it was nationalist separatist terrorist organizations such as the IRA and Chechen rebels who were behind most attacks. The number of incidents from nationalist separatist groups has remained stable in the years since, while religious extremism has grown. The prevalence of Islamic groups in Iraq, Afghanistan, Pakistan, Nigeria and Syria is the main driver behind these trends.

Four of the terrorist groups that have been most active since 2001 are Boko Haram, Al Qaeda, the

Taliban and ISIL. These groups have been most active in Iraq, Afghanistan, Pakistan, Nigeria, and Syria. Eighty percent of all deaths from terrorism occurred in one of these five countries.

And that's what I have to offer on this subject. I hope it will be of value to you in some way, and now we must bid you good-bye and good luck."

The applause was piercing and sustained.

Rick gave the chief his phone number along with a hearty thank you. Then he and his triad headed for Hungary. On the way, Rick tried to dislodge some of the past hour from his mind but was unsuccessful … until he happened to envision a haggard Napoleon Bonaparte! Somehow, Napoleon and Dracula occupied a bicameral position in his mind:

—Admiration for Napoleon? Yes. Why would I devote a whole book to this man if I didn't feel this way?

—Existence of a real Dracula? Yes and no.

The Dracula one was easy to understand because Rick was currently "living it". Not so in the case of Napoleon, however, because that meant ancient history. Nonetheless, he often read about him and even wrote about him in one of his books. While on the flight to Budapest, he took out *The Strange Death of Napoleon Bonaparte* from his satchel and as he was likening his repeated readings to the endless receipt of his phone calls, he remembered writing about a specific Napoleon diary entry. One that reflected dejection while sitting as an exile in St. Helena. In it, he referred to himself as "Napoleon", not as "I" or "me". Rick labeled its words somewhat of a grand proclamation and once said to a friend who was about to read it: “It must have taken him weeks to put this all together, and it may seem like more than weeks before you reach the end of it, but here it is.” And the friend read it:

You want to know the treasures of Napoleon? They are enormous, it is true, but in full view. Here they are: the splendid harbour of Antwerp, that of Flushing, capable of holding the largest fleets; the docks and dykes of Dunkirk, of Havre, of Nice; the gigantic harbour of Cherbourg; the harbour works at Venice; the great roads from Antwerp to Amsterdam, from Mainz to Metz, from Bordeaux to Bayonne; the passes of the Simplon, of Mont Cenis, of Mont Genevre, of the Corniche, that gave four openings through the Alps; in that alone, you might reckon 800 millions. The roads from the Pyrenees to the Alps, from Parma to Spezzia, from Savona to Piedmont; the bridges of Jena, of Austerlitz, of the Arts, of Sèvres, of Tours, of Lyons, of Turin, of the Isère, of the Durance, of Bordeaux, of Rouen; the canal from the Rhine to the Rhone, joining the waters of Holland to the Mediterranean; the canal that joins the Scheldt and the Somme, connecting Amsterdam and Paris; that which joins the Rance and the Vilaine; the canal of the Arles, of Pavia, of the Rhine; the draining of the marshes of Bourgoing, of the citentin, of Rochefort; the rebuilding of most of the churches pulled down during the Revolution, the building of new ones; the construction of many industrial establishments for putting an end to pauperism; the construction of the Louvre, of the public graneries, of the Bank, of the canal of the Ourcq; the

> water system of the city of Paris, the numerous sewers, the quays, the embellishments and monuments of Lyons. Fifty millions spent on repairing and improving the Crown residences; sixty millions' worth of furniture placed in the palaces of France and Holland, at Turin, at Rome; sixty millions' worth of Crown diamonds, all of it the money of Napoleon; even the Regent, the only missing one of the old diamonds of the Crown of France, purchased from Berlin Jews with whom it was pledged for three millions; the Napoleon Museum, valued at more than 400 millions. These are monuments to confound calumny. History will relate that all this was accomplished in the midst of continuous wars, without raising a loan, and with the public debt actually decreasing day by day.

After having written the book about the life of Napoleon, it was difficult for Rick to separate the emperor's activities from the ongoing Dracula/Milosevic saga. Angela had even commented on it over the phone. He had put in the call to her while still on the plane.

"But at least," she had said, "it creates a neutralizing effect during the ups and downs of what you're now writing about."

"Good point, my dear, but I'm completely bothered. It's about all I've heard and read regarding the role of arsenic in Napoleon's life. He and his troops used a small amount as a recreational drug on a regular basis. They had no idea about a cumulative effect. Could it have been slipped to him in larger quantities? Or the wall paper in the room he slept in for years at St. Helena. The paint in the paper had arsenic in it. Could he have been breathing it? That diary entry is long and complicated but in addition to that, I think it smells of a guy who's gone loopy. And I don't like that it tainted some of his merits … like his building of new churches and his getting rid of pauperism. Not to mention his military successes. I've got to review them one of these days."

It didn't take long, for within the hour he yanked the Napoleon book out of his satchel again and read what he had once written. He could have said most of the words internally but he wanted to be accurate about both the emperor's many successes and the gradual evolution of mistakes:

> First off, Napoleon had a natural grasp of the essential tactics of war and the art of waging it. He would rattle off these aphorisms as if they were golden rules and early in his career they pretty much were. Like, "A field of battle which the enemy has previously studied and reconnoitered should be avoided," or, "March dispersed, fight concentrated", or, "When it is possible to employ thunderbolts, their use should be preferred to that of cannon". And my favorite: "War is an immense art which comprises all others. It is also, like politics, a matter of tact." Rick formed the words like an evangelistic preacher. "There's almost a pious glory to them," he said, "but eventually Napoleon blasphemed that glory. Take the first one about reconnoitering. He broke it by attacking Wellington on the Waterloo position even though the Duke had reconnoitered it the year before. And Napoleon knew it. Now then, along about 1812, during the Russian Campaign specifically, things began to change. His mechanics of warfare became flawed and that continued on until his pitiful fall at Waterloo three years later. That period was not Napoleon's finest … what an understatement! For in a way, the real Napoleon ceased to exist. I won't much elaborate but during those two debacles and during the Spanish and French campaigns, he violated the classic maneuvers of warfare. Most military experts say there are only seven of them. To wit: penetration of the center, envelopment of a single

> flank, envelopment of both flanks, attack in oblique order, the feigned withdrawal, attack from a defensive position, and the indirect approach. But without a doubt, the worst thing he ever said, and a dead giveaway that his mind was being altered, was, 'I have fought sixty battles and I have learnt nothing that I did not know in the beginning.' Can you imagine? Learnt nothing! Have I made my case about the gradual poisoning of one of the greatest military commanders in history … right up there with Alexander and Caesar?

That night, Rick spent an hour writing about the day's activities in book form, just as Leon had requested of him. Vérité's chairman was, in turn, following the request of the movie mogul. The activities included:

—Arriving in Belgrade, Serbia

—Reading about the country

—Meeting with Chief Hassel and asking for his assistance

—Giving a talk on terrorism

—About Napoleon Bonaparte

—His complex dairy entry

Chapter 4

One of Rick's favorite cities was Budapest, Hungary's capital city, and it was there that they would next venture. They landed at the Ferihegy International Airport and waiting for Ansel to rent a car, Rick read through a poster:

> Our Hungary is a small, landlocked country here in central Europe. Great economic and social changes have occurred since the late 1940s. Before that time, most of our country's income came from agriculture and the majority of Hungarians lived in rural areas and worked on farms. But the country's economy has become increasingly industrialized. Almost a fifth of our population live here in Budapest where, despite such changes, people still love highly seasoned foods, excellent wines and lively folk music for which we have long been famous.
>
> Our chief agricultural products are wheat, corn, milk, potatoes, grapes, chickens and eggs. And our chief manufacturing products are steel, railroad equipment, electrical goods, pharmaceuticals and textiles.
>
> The Danube River cuts right through this capital city which is often called the "Queen of the Danube". We are made up of Buda and Pest, the former containing famous public buildings and green hills; the latter, wide avenues and large shopping centers.
>
> Welcome and do enjoy your stay here.

Rick was walking toward the rented car when, up ahead, a larger one streaked past it and disappeared up a side street, only to return in his direction, this time more slowly. When it passed him, it stopped for a moment, then streaked away. Rick couldn't make out anything about the driver, for the car's windows were dark. He wondered if the episode … lasting less than a minute … had any significance, but with his talk about to take place, he dismissed it as a coincidence.

What then transpired happened to be a mirror image of the Belgrade visit including a high school assembly hall and a police chief, Fritz Elser, who was just as flowery in his introduction of Rick, and an audience of students that was just as boisterous until Rick began to speak. This time, however, they all rose while clapping.

After a lasting smile Rick began:

> "Thank you all. Now I'll go about this in a special mythological way. And what could be more like that than to give a talk titled, 'The Myth of Mythology'? No one laughed and Rick thought they just didn't get it, so he simply carried on. "Anyway," he said, "let me take you through that subject, and I'll be reading directly from notes I put together before writing a book that included mythology. Also … I'll be using American lingo and titles in some of this, and I hope you either understand them or are not thrown off by them"
>
> > There's a general misconception that myths arose simply to entertain … yesterday's equivalent of *The Sopranos*, let's say. But that's only part of the story.
> >
> > For they lead us back to a time when the world was young and people had a connection with the earth and nature … with trees and flowers and hills and seas … unlike anything we ourselves can feel now. In other words, through myths, we can retrace the paths from today's civilized man who lives so far from nature, to man who lived so close to it.

Now the link between myths and nature is only *one* aspect of what mythology is all about. The general public has, by and large, put its *own* spin on them … most people dismissing mythology as a pack of silly stories that were (1) made up and (2) insignificant. That's only partly correct. Made up? Yes. Insignificant? No.

For myths were explanations made long ago … before science came into vogue … to understand what people were witnessing. Things like lightning, and changes of season, and love, and hate, and death.

And they used gods and heroes and monsters and demons and witches to tell the tales. It was the best that humans could do at the time, because they couldn't provide scientific explanations for any of this.

Natural events as well as human behavior, all came to be understood through tales of gods, goddesses, and heroes. Thunder, earthquakes, eclipses, rain, and the success of crops were all due to the intervention of powerful gods.

The Greeks believed that, at one time, all the world's evils and problems were trapped inside a box. When this box was opened by the first woman, all the world's misfortunes escaped before she was able to close the lid. They called her Pandora. "Opening Pandora's Box".

So myths can be a powerful business … and that's one reason they've been around for so long … since a time when the world was full of danger, mystery, and wonder. As if it isn't now!

In most of my talks, I usually cover present day mysteries, true crime and forensic science. But now, for what I guess you'd call a dramatic change of pace, I'd like to elaborate for just a few minutes on the *importance* of mythology … something I've always been intrigued with, never fully understood, and only recently appreciated in terms of its place in the history of civilization.

And I'll confine my remarks to two areas:

One — the *impact* of myths on our culture

And two — their *role in history* .

So let's start with #1: the *impact* of myths — not only those of Greece and Rome — but also those about Norse gods such as Thor and Egyptian gods who inspired the pyramids, for example.

These myths and those from many other civilizations continue to fascinate millions of people, many of whom don't label the whole process as mythology.

Some call it "Going to the Movies". For example, consider: The Lord of the Rings trilogy; Troy; E.T.; and above all, Star Wars. All these draw on mythic themes.

Think about this one. There are ancient tales of so-called trickster gods who were greedy, mischievous, and evil … kind of like the Joker in Batman, really.

Often they took animal form, like the African Rabbit or Native American Coyote. Sounds like Bugs Bunny and his nemesis, Willy Coyote to me!

And it's not just the entertainment industry that's capitalized on myths. How about Halloween … a modern version of an ancient mythical celebration?

In fact, many of the trappings of Christmas, including Christmas trees, wreaths, mistletoe, holly and ivy, are borrowed from ancient traditions of Northern Europe in which the evergreen symbolized the hope for new life in the dead of winter.

To get another gauge of the impact of myths:

Check the calendar: the names of all the days and months derive from Greek, Roman and Norse mythology.

Check the planets in our solar system: all except Earth are named for Roman gods.

Check our language: loaded with words from our mythic past: Do you buy books from Amazon.com? Are you wearing a pair of Nikes? How about words like panacea, hypnosis, panic, morphine, leprechaun, typhoon. hurricane?

Myths certainly surround us in literature, in pop culture, and in our language.

Next we have #2: *History.* Myths also play a serious role here. In wartime Japan, for example, they were the source of the national Shinto religion, for the Japanese emperor Hirohito was supposedly descended from a Shinto sun goddess. This devotion to the emperor led to the use of the notorious kamikaze pilots with their dynamite-laden planes and their suicide crashes into U.S. warships. It was a myth/religion that drove these young men … and an entire nation … with fanatical devotion to its emperor.

And of course, it doesn't end there as more recent history has shown. I'm talking about 9/11. The notion of dying a martyr's death and gaining entrance to a paradise with the promise of virgins is an enticing idea that continues to drive the terrorists who strap explosives to their bodies, or drive cars filled with explosives, or fly hijacked jets into buildings. They're motivated by beliefs whose roots stretch back centuries ago … the idea of warriors gaining entrance to paradise through early death is certainly not exclusive to any one mythology or faith.

We might even say that one person's "myth" is another person's "religion".

The history of myth, in other words, goes hand in hand with the history of civilization. Stop and think about "ancient civilization." What does it mean? The wheel. Writing. Bronze. Glass. Fireworks. Paper. Noodles. In-door plumbing. Beer. These are only a few of the pleasant and delightful creations devised by the ancient civilizations of Egypt, China, Greece, India, Rome, and others.

These civilizations also gave us astronomy, democracy, and philosophy.

Now you're probably thinking, "Wait a minute. All you're doing is listing various discoveries."

Yes, I am, but here's the important point. These same ancients "invented" the myths that grew hand in hand with the discoveries of their civilizations, making it impossible to separate one from the other. That is, to separate out myths from history itself. So while the importance of myths may seem less obvious than that of the wheel, writing, or a mug of beer, these old stories are still a dominant force in our lives today. They remain alive in our literature, our language, the theater, dreams, psychology, and various religions.

In a way, then, myths helped *make* civilization.

And to repeat myself but to say it in a different way: myths began so that humans could explain and describe the world they could see as well as the world they only imagined existed … that is, the world they couldn't see.

I'm talking long before science envisioned the Big Bang. Long before philosophers reasoned or sought enlightenment. Long before Darwin proposed natural selection. Long before we could know the age of a rock and before men walked on the moon. They explained how Europe was created; where life came from; why the stars shine at night and the seasons change; why there was sex; why there was evil; why people died and where they went when they did.

In short, myths were a very human way to explain *everything* and, in so doing, they've given us a sweeping and stimulating view of the world.

Finally, what are the differences between myth, legend, fable, folktale and fairy tale?

Myths usually involve gods — supernatural beings who actually controlled events in the natural world.

Legends, on the other hand, are really an early form of history — stories about historical figures, usually humans, not gods, that are handed down from earlier times. Most Americans, for instance, understand the story of George Washington and the cherry tree. A legend.

Fables are simple, usually brief, fictitious stories, typically teaching a moral, or making a cautionary point or satirizing human behavior. In many fables, the moral is usually told at the end, in the form of a proverb. Often, they feature animals that speak and act like human beings, as in the most famous examples … those attributed to Aesop as in *Aesop's Fables*. Stories like *The Turtle and the Hare*, in which slow and steady wins the race. That's the moral there. Or *The Grasshopper and the Ant* in which a fun-loving but lazy grasshopper plays while the ant dutifully stores away food for the winter. There's a moral there, too.

Folktales are stories usually handed down orally and are meant to entertain, not instruct. They usually tell of the customs, superstitions and beliefs of ordinary people … so they usually don't involve gods.

Fairy Tales are usually filled with elves, pixies, fairies and other supernatural creatures with magical powers. In both folktales and fairy tales, the central character tends to be a person of low stature, frequently trapped in a case of mistaken identity, who has been victimized or persecuted, like Cinderella by her wicked step-sisters.

The best known examples of folk and fairy tales are the tales of *Arabian Nights*, including *Ali Baba and the Forty Thieves*, *Aladdin's Lamp*, and *Sinbad the Sailor*. Another famous collection is *Grimm's Fairy Tales* which includes *Hansel and Gretal*, *Little Red Riding Hood, Snow White, and Sleeping Beauty*. Many of these were drawn from much older, mythic sources.

Well, that's just been a glimpse of mythology. I'll end by reading what I once wrote: "Myths have been the precursors to many important things we take for granted today. Things that in their original form, people of centuries ago wondered about and made up stories about. But beyond that, people everywhere love … or perhaps need … to create a good story. And if the details

> change a bit in the retelling, what's the difference? Who among us hasn't stretched the truth with a touch of dramatic flair to add some color and spice to an encounter at the supermarket or an argument with the boss? Often, these stories … just like everyday rumors and tabloid-newspaper reports … change with every retelling. It has always been that way, and always will be. So it is that the myths of every culture include all these other types of 'stories' … legends, fables, folktales and fairy tales. It's really been a neat arrangement … one that's given us a sweeping and stimulating view of the world."

Thank you and good luck.

No sooner had Rick finished bowing during a prolonged applause than he felt his phone vibrating at the hip. He moved off to the side, pressed the earpiece to his head and spoke softly.

"Yes?"

It was Angela and she sounded upset. "Rick," she said, "You've **got** to come home! Someone threw a large rock through our living room window. It had a piece of paper tied around it and it read, 'Stop. We are after you'."

"What? Did you call the police?"

"Yes, but please come home."

"What did the police do?"

"One officer came, looked up and down the street, hardly spoke to me and then he left. Please, please come home!" This time she shouted.

"Now listen," Rick said, "I will, but I'm nine hours away. Here's what you do, Ange. Call David Brooks at Hollings; have him call the police back, make sure they patrol the area thoroughly and have David stay with you until I get there. He packs two guns just like me. Got it?"

"Yes. But when will you leave?"

"I'll inform the others and then we'll head for the airport. I doubt they'll hang around without me. No more visits by **me** around here though … that's for sure. And who do I think is behind what happened? Maybe the Dracula people … who knows?"

Screw Dracula. Screw Milosevic. Even screw Napoleon.
And screw the movie business.

Fran, Leon and Ansel had heard Rick's end of the conversation and after Rick slammed the phone back to his hip, Leon asked, "A problem?"

"More than that. A problem and a change of plans. A **complete** change."

He then informed the triad about what Angela had said and indicated he wanted to head home … immediately. They said they'd follow suit, though Fran added that he'd be available whenever Rick needed him.

In a separate sense, Rick was relieved … not at all by the phone call … but because of sheer exhaustion and an increasing disinterest in the Balkan schedule. He thought the triad also looked relieved, but he was in no mood to ask about it.

"So we'll cancel what the future was to hold here and we'll all go home," Leon said. "But when things get cleared up there … hopefully … we'll return here … right?"

"Maybe."

"That does it," Rick said to himself. It hadn't fully dawned on him at the start, but now he came to the conclusion that the Dracula/Milosevic mission had ceased to exist. That it had given way to a different one … a new chapter in his life that was more thought provoking, more personal … but more dangerous.

If not the Dracula camp, then who is after me and why?

He hadn't dwelled on something as long as he did now: if the Dracula-type person wanted to be rid of me because he felt either that I was on to him or that I might hurt their business in the long run … the one that Alex handles … why take so long?

Chapter 5

After landing at Bradley Airport in Connecticut, Rick doled out sixty dollars for a taxi drive to his New Haven home.

He stumbled through the front door. Angela and David were seated at the kitchen table, having coffee and left-over doughnuts.

Rick rushed to embrace his wife and kiss her.

"Thank God," she whispered in his ear as she forced herself up, still clutching him. She handed him the paper containing the warning message. He read it quickly and pocketed it, thinking that later he might examine it for trace and transfer evidence.

Rick then broke away and gave David just as long an embrace before pulling away. "Thank you, my man," Rick said, "but no kiss."

All three gave the kind of nervous laugh that so often accompanies thankful situations.

They moved to the living room and sat down on easy chairs which they had dragged into a circle. During a short silence and an even shorter glance at one another, David said, "You know, Rick, in addition to my being a medical doctor, I've been the head of the security team at Hollings General for how long now? Over twenty years? And you were part of it, too. Remind me: when did you leave us?

"Six years ago on the button."

"But I never knew why you left in the first place, so I'll ask you now."

Rick's answer was immediate. "Because I wanted to travel and sightsee. But no more. No more. I'd work out of Hollings as long as they'd have me. It's where I belong, really. Doesn't mean I wouldn't travel to get things done. Anywhere in the world, in fact, as long as it doesn't involve the Balkans, and especially Transylvania. In fact, I wouldn't be surprised if I'd be spending a week or more in visiting foreign countries. But I'd want the other end to know that I represented Hollings."

He next gave a brief description of what he had been going through in the Balkans and that, under the circumstances, he was not disappointed in surrendering all of it. "Every last damn bit of it."

"Maybe this isn't the time to bring this up, Rick, but we've had kind of a security problem at the hospital. I don't really understand it fully but our administrator does. He could explain it to you. Any chance you could be with us again? Your old office is still unoccupied."

"The Hole?"

"The Hole."

Rick twisted his lips into a smile.

"And is Terry Foster still your administrator?"

David nodded. Then he said, "I can tell you he'd like to have you back. We often talk about it."

Rick had never expected such an invitation, said so, and followed with: "let me think on it, Dave, and I'll call you. Right now, I need more sleep, a shower, and maybe more than anything else … buying a new car."

Moments before David left, he said he understood Rick's decision about not rushing things and would wait to hear back from him.

David saluted Rick at the doorway. He saluted back but Angela blew a kiss toward Hollings' head of security.

The two Chandlers then spoke little as they returned to one of the chairs and Angela sat on Rick's lap for a spell. He nearly fell asleep until she nudged him into their retiring for the night.

Chapter 6

In the morning, the first thing Rick did after a hurried breakfast was to drive Angela's Chevy to the Northwest Auto Dealership. There, he became impressed with a certain car after spending only ten minutes in an enormous display room. He had run his hands over its outside; sat on its driver and passenger sides; inspected under its hood and in its trunk; and kicked all four tires. Finally, an employee tagged along in the Chevy as Rick began a test run in the new one. They drove by his house to drop off the Chevy after which the employee joined Rick in the new car.

On their return to Northwest Auto, he bought the Mercedes Benz. It was a four-door black sedan.

Rick made the rounds thanking more than that single employee, as if they had all saved his life. Next, he drove to the nearest car wash for he had once heard that prospective buyers would all run their hands over new cars on display. Just like himself, ten minutes earlier.

It cost ten dollars at the car wash and he added tips for the men on each side of the Mercedes. Then, he sat with the car in "neutral" and his foot off the gas pedal. As it slid along the narrow lane of water and soapy drizzle banging against the car's windows and wheels, a single question emerged in his mind: Was David serious about the offer of returning to Hollings?

Once home, he planned on calling David to find out. Earlier, while anticipating that purchasing a car wouldn't take much time, he had left a note for Angela on the kitchen table. It read:

> Please go to work, Ange. Things will work out. I dreamed about going back to work at the hospital but not for a day or two. We'll see.

He tore up the note and tossed it in a waste basket. Then he went into their bedroom, shook Angela awake, and told her about the new car. After she freshened up, he led her into their garage to see it.

"It's gorgeous!" she exclaimed, "and I have an idea, my darling."

"What's that?"

"Why don't you use the Chevy and I'll use this one."

He nearly choked her and said, "No way, José."

"Just thought I'd try," she said.

"Okay. So that's the car. Now for Hollings. I've already decided to return there if David was sincere in asking me to. He's already said that Foster would like me back. The idea of waiting around and doing nothing except watching T.V. and maybe writing some is crazy. I'd soon become a couch potato."

"I don't think Dave was kidding, Rick, and I'm happy for you."

"But it's not quite 9:30 yet and that's when he usually gets there, even on a Saturday, so I'll wait before calling."

He sipped on another cup of coffee while browsing through the morning newspaper that had been delivered inside the front screen door. But nothing really sunk in for he was only wasting time until 9:30 or so rolled around. He hoped that David was in his office by then.

At 9:40, Angela left for some weekend work after planting a kiss on Rick's forehead. He was dialing a call to David's office.

"Morning, Dave. You sitting down?"

"Yeah, why? What's wrong?"

"Nothing's wrong. I've decided to take you up on the offer. If you meant it, I can arrive there by noon."

There was a pause that, to Rick, seemed like ages. Finally, David said, "Sorry about that. I had to catch my breath. But that's fantastic with a capital F !"

"You're sure there's enough for me to do?"

"Plenty."

"And you said my Hole is still available?"

"Sure is. We can clean it up and you can move in as soon as you arrive."

That done, Rick folded his hands behind his head and leaned back in a recliner. He remembered a time when life seemed simpler. When rivers and trees and flying butterflies meant more to him. When he even *noticed* them more than now. Or when there were workers for every job that needed doing — on the roads, atop telephone poles, on the farms, in the factories. Not any more thinking like that, however, for now all of life had become more complicated. And he wasn't alone in such thinking, for columnists and T.V. commentators offered similar opinions on a regular basis. But as he straightened up, he was content in blaming such dalliance on his becoming not necessarily wiser, but older.

Chapter 7

At noon, Rick left for Hollings General Teaching Hospital. It was an 800 bed complex surrounded by oak trees and evergreens. And the Police Department Building was only a block away.

Rick's approach to the hospital involved driving down a steep hill. He hadn't done so in six years but, at the start, the memory of it made him feel that many years younger.

His eyes caught its commanding clock tower, a reflex he was certain all visitors shared. He slowed up to admire the hundred-year-old structure, a continuation of the elevator shaft still in use for the administrative section of the complex. Half again as tall, it sported silent clocks on three sides, shaded by a copper cupola. And, in Rick's mind, it pierced the sky like a foundation pile in reverse. Architecturally, it was the only feature of the hospital he liked. Tested and timeless amidst a mishmash of wings and additions, red brick against greys and tans and glass.

Inside, there was an acute care section, a chronic care section and the Glendale Entertainment Center. The latter was larger than two basketball courts. Besides a nurses' station, it had a stage and podium; card tables and wheel chairs ; and countered windows through which kitchen personnel offered light foods. Backgrounded in soft music, it was always filled with patients from the chronic care section who were nearing their discharges.

Rick marched straight to David's office. "Here I am," Rick said. "Ready or not."

"Glad you're back. I hadn't realized how much people missed you until I spread the word that you'd be returning. And you know what they missed the most, aside from your security skills?

"No, what?"

"The talks you used to give over at the Entertainment Center about practically anything, but especially scientific matters. I'll never forget the one on forensic science, or even the essay you once wrote about "Jack the Ripper".

"Hmm, maybe I should start them up again. I'm a show-off, you know."

"No you're not, and I'm certain they'd be well received again."

"We'll see."

A lull preceded what David finally said: "Well, let me get something out of the way, Rick. I'll be sixty-five next month and it's time for me to phase out."

"Phase out?"

"Yeah. To retire. That is, from here. To be blunt about it … and I hope I'm not discouraging you, but I've grown tired of the staggering stacks of paper work, from the annoyances of dealing with insurance companies and Health Maintenance organizations, and from other elements in the increasing Managed Care approach to medicine. But I don't want to abandon patient care altogether. The solution then would be to restrict my medical practice to making house calls for other doctors. I've always enjoyed that. You can then take over security here … completely on your own. You up to it?"

Rick, taken by surprise, sat down and stared at his shoes. Then he arose, walked slowly to a window and raised its shade. He looked out beyond the trees, back at David, then beyond the trees again.

"Hello!" David exclaimed. "You still here?"

Rick adjusted and readjusted his tie before clearing his throat and replying: “So you’re about to phase out, and I’d be about to phase in.”

“That’s it, and I repeat: I hope I haven’t discouraged you.”

“Not at all.”

While receiving the news, Rick couldn’t help but ferret out the warning note that had been tossed through his living room window. And coupled with that thought was a brief one that sent chills up his spine.

Contact that guy in Transylvania about it? Ridiculous!
Couldn’t deal with him right now, anyway.

He felt seized with a combination of thoughts that seemed unrelated. Or maybe they were:

—His leaving Transylvania

—David’s leaving the hospital

—Someone leaving a warning note.

They shook hands, saluted one another, and shook hands again.

Chapter 8

Meantime, David left his position at the hospital. Rick had apologized for something he said that was none of his business, and had even helped in putting David's belongings together and taking them out to his car.

"I'll be on call for you any time," David had said through his car's window.

"And the same here," Rick had replied. "Let's hope I'm not a bother to you."

He returned home to tidy himself up before spending time with Administrator Foster. It was about the noon hour and daylight had a time of it, the sun in full display through a sheet of white clouds. All the more reason for him not to notice a light that was shining through the living room window. He shielded his eyes to be certain. And it was there all right. But why? Had he forgotten to switch it off before leaving the house, or was there another reason? One that made him whip out his shoulder pistol. He slid out of his Mercedes, quietly closed its door and sneaked over to a side entrance to the garage. It was empty, so Angela had not returned from work. He then entered the house through a back door and yelled out, "Anyone here?"

There was no answer, so he returned the pistol to its holster and switched off the light, both upset and relieved that he had forgotten to switch off *all* lights before earlier leaving the house.

When he returned to the hospital, he nearly knocked over a fire extinguisher as he leaned against a wall. He never felt confident in making decisions while walking. The decision to be made was about first checking the Hole or first conferring with Foster. It was Hole before Foster. Rick hoped to be happy with his old "office" and then also with some time spent with his old boss who, in addition to offering a warm welcome, might elaborate on the "security problem" that David had touched upon.

The Hole was located off a corridor on the basement level next to an equipment room, not far from the old elevator. It was nothing more than a tiny space with a door and had ratty walls, a ratty ceiling and a ratty cement floor. At the top of the corridor, flaking cream pipes came at the door from both sides and snaked through its header to fan out above a desk and three chairs inside. The pipes which Rick had sworn were sheathed in unreported asbestos, ran through two cellar-like windows on the outer wall, apparently into a rear corridor. He had often wondered what in hell he was doing in such a rattrap. And for some strange reason, part of that wonderment included a "why-with-all", a phrase he had long ago coined. He believed it to be a catchy phrase and determined that it stemmed from the hospital's accepting and solving so many problems — medical and otherwise — over decades and decades. His "why-with-all", in turn, may have been fueled by a newspaper the hospital published - - - at first monthly, and now bi-weekly. Titled *The Hollings Times*, it offered commentary and/or help that ranged from nutrition to scientific advances; from sleeping disorders to sexual harassment charges; from criminal activity to the prevention of cybercrime. The paper was distributed without charge throughout the state and to a few other parts of New England. In Rick's eyes, all of this represented a medical care facility being combined with an information superhighway where people, near and far, could seek and receive assistance of all sorts. All they needed to do was to contact the hospital's front office and spell out their request. Such requests were handled by what was termed the "Question Division".

The catchy phrase, the newspaper coverage and Rick's view of the hospital dominated his thinking as he smelled medicinal and detergent crosscurrents from the pharmacy and laundry on an opposite end of the corridor. Often, when he dashed from the Hole, he would freeze in his tracks to avert the daily caravan of laundry carts. Yet not of employees, for nearly none had ever been in the area.

But now, everything looked clean and polished and something new had been added: a picture on the wall. It had been taken eight years before and was of the senior hospital staff, including Rick. His hair was longer and he wore glasses, not contact lenses.

Next was Foster's office on the second floor. As Rick left the Hole, he looked at its door and thought he'd arrange for a tablet to be fastened to its outer side. It would read: SECURITY and COMPLIANCE.

The administrator *did* offer a warm welcome. "It's been six years of missing you," he said. "You and all you've done for us."

"And there's not enough time to tell you how much I've missed this place," Rick stated. "We started here together about 20 years ago. Remember?"

The mutual compliments and some story-telling took about half an hour and then Rick came right out and asked about the security problem.

"It's a problem that involves "Managed Care" to a degree. And indirectly," Foster said. "Bottom line is that a percentage of monies we receive for services rendered here has been siphoned off to unknown parties. And that it's been going on for some time but was only recently discovered."

"I see," Rick said. "Well, it better head my list of things to tackle, right after I get settled. Off hand, it sounds like diverted money leading to money laundering."

Over the next two days, he made the rounds of the hospital, talking with familiar staff members including doctors, nurses, lab technicians, the ambulance crew, library personnel and other employees. He also decided to check a small turret in his house. It was used specifically for his gun collection, the one he had started when they rented their Bridgeport apartment. He had taken along all his gun cabinets, their metallic odor kept unchecked by glass doors. He kept the cabinets stocked the same as before — all sizes, all heights, all filled. There was a cabinet overflowing with weapons according to manufacturer: Colt, Ruger, Smith and Wesson, Charter Arms, Dan Wesson. According to calibers: .25, .32, .38, .45. Cabinets for pistols, for revolvers, for rifles and carbines and machine guns and shotguns and knives. One of the largest cabinets was stuffed with spare parts and all varieties of ammunition. Three others contained various papers and folders that had been thrown in over the years.

He had often taken different guns to High Rock Firing Range where he spent time refreshing his skills. And just as often, he took Angela along to instruct her on how to deal with her own Beretta Cougar .45. It hadn't taken long before she became gun-savvy and kept it hidden in her purse.

There was no intention of replacing the weapons that were regularly at his shoulder and ankle, but being in the turret for a few minutes would somehow give him an added measure of overall security. He had even toyed with a question before sauntering among the collection: "There is no logic to it, but why not envision hospital security with my own **personal** security?"

Chapter 9

Since his return was ushered in with many friendly hugs, Rick thought he could match them with an early talk on day three. He asked to have a gooseneck microphone turned on at the pulpit of the Glendale Entertainment Center and to have as many of staff personnel squeezed in there. This all coincided with a hospital-wide public address announcement of the talk.

When the time came, Terry Foster volunteered to introduce him, but Rick refused. Instead, he walked to the podium and said:

"Greetings everybody. As most of you know by now, I'm happy to be back."

He hadn't expected it, but the applause that followed was as loud as the clang of a fire truck.

"Thank you," he continued. "Now I'm about to give the same talk I gave here some six years ago. And, as I did then, I'll read directly from notes with very little off-the-cuff remarks." He held up a manila folder.

"I'll be covering, number one, *Forensic Science*. Number two, *DNA*. Number three, an essay I wrote about *Jack the Ripper*. And finally, I'll end with some humor."

He placed the folder on the podium, whipped it open with a flourish, and began:

"The most concise definition I could put together of forensic science is that it's the application of the biological, chemical, and physical sciences to matters involving the law. There was a time when forensic science and criminalistics were considered one and the same, but not anymore. It's sort of an oxymoron, but forensic science has both expanded and contracted. Expanded by having more disciplines under its umbrella and contracted because of specialization.

"Imagine forensic science as an umbrella. Down its center is a pole … its core. A core that is still criminalistics. And what's its definition? Well, it deals with crime scenes — with the recognition, collection, identification, preservation, and interpretation of physical evidence at crime scenes. It also includes crime scene reconstruction.

"Now criminalistics has its own subdivisions that sprout out from the bottom of the pole. Think of any field and put 'forensic' in front of it, and it currently exists:

—forensic medicine

—forensic odontology (dentistry)

—forensic anthropology (skeletal remains)

—forensic entomology (the life cycle of insects to help pinpoint the time of death)

—forensic engineering

—forensic nursing.

"And I'll leave forensic science at that. Now for a few words about DNA. It stands for deoxy-ribo-nucleic acid. It's the stuff of life and distinguishes one individual from another. You from me, and us from the rest of the world. But identical twins have the same DNA. It's present in every one of the 100 trillion cells of the body. Imagine a cell wall. It's filled with cytoplasm and embedded in the cytoplasm is a nucleus. But there are also two other genetic materials there in the nucleus: chromosomes and genes. There are 23 pairs of chromosomes … one set from one's mother, and one set from one's father. The chromosomes carry the genes. So they carry the genes and the genes are made up of DNA.

"The thing that boggles my mind is: if the function of a cell is to act as a miniature factory under the command of DNA, and it's the same DNA throughout the body, how come a heart cell knows enough to pump blood rather than do arithmetic? One of the great mysteries!

"Finally, let's get to the *Jack the Ripper* essay. It's a relatively short one that I once wrote for a magazine on forensic science.

> The time was a nine week period in the fall of 1888, sometimes referred to as "The Autumn of Terror".
>
> The place was the Whitechapel district of London. That was the *east* end. Where the slums were. Where prostitutes flourished.
>
> Jack the Ripper. Few names in history are as instantly recognizable. Fewer still, evoke such vivid images: noisy courts and alleys, cabs and gaslights, swirly fog, prostitutes decked out in the tawdriest of finery, the shrill cry of newsboys … and silent, cruel death personified in the cape-shrouded figure of a faceless prowler of the night, armed with a long knife and carrying a Gladstone bag. And his identity is still unknown, although there is hardly a year in the 132 since, when a new brainstorm doesn't emerge. When experts don't continue to speculate. I won't dwell on the many aspects of this saga. It would take all day. But I'll list a few:

1—The homicides themselves, at least five, usually with terrible brutalization.

2—The victims, all female prostitutes.

3—The investigation—intense, prolonged.

4—The endless theories.

5—The abundance of graffiti.

6—The varied letters and postcards, some considered authentic (that is, sent by the killer) but most considered hoaxes.

7—The suspects: a mad doctor, a professional butcher, a deranged mid-wife, a mysterious lodger, even a member of royalty.

Actually, so much of the Ripper is mired in mystery and myth. And, with the passage of time, much can get (1) exaggerated, (2) embellished upon, or (3) otherwise distorted.

I have a simple way of viewing such things: "The older the story, the more grains of salt it should be taken with."

So here goes. It's not very long. Quite concise, in fact. I'll just devote a page or two to why the Ripper continues to be discussed. To give you a sense of what it was all about. I must emphasize, first and foremost, that Jack the Ripper created the myth, representing the archetype of the more modern serial killer. This isn't to say that the whole story is a myth, just that the story has been one of mythical proportions.

By today's standards of crime, *Jack the Ripper* would barely make international headlines. I mean: COME ON!

(1) The murder of five prostitutes in a slum swarming with criminals?
(2) Just one more violent creep satisfying his perverted needs?
(3) No, hardly anyone would be incensed over the fate of those five prostitutes as were the respectable families and friends of the pretty college students who were Ted Bundy's victims. At least 30 here in the United States.
(4) Unfortunately, we've become a society numbed by horrible crimes inflicted upon many victims, especially in the last dozen years or so.

Why then, are there still stories and songs and operas and movies and a never-ending stream of books about this one Victorian criminal?

Why are there many Ripperologists and no Bundyologists?

> Why is the Ripper story as popular today as it was in Victorian London?

For two main reasons: First, because *Jack the Ripper* represents the classic whodunit. The story has a terrifying, almost supernatural quality. It's been said that he came out of the fog, killed violently by slashing a throat from ear to ear, and quickly disappeared without a trace. And after his last victim was found, he vanished from the face of the earth. Forever.

But over time, much has been distorted and that brings us to the second reason for its continued fascination: mis-impression. In spite of their barbarism, the murders represent a real-life mystery from the era of Sherlock Holmes … the late 1880s … the bygone, romantic era of high Victorian society, with gaslights and swirling London fog. But get this! Not one single killing took place on a foggy night. Not one single killing had any real relationship to Victorian splendor.

Plus, of all possible coincidences, at the same time these murders were occurring, guess what was thrilling audiences across town at the Lyceum Theatre, in the fashionable west end? *The Strange Case of Dr. Jekyl and Mr. Hyde.*

Together … these two things — a classic whodunit and the Jekyl and Hyde coincidence … gave many people their first awareness of the potential for inherent evil in so-called normal individuals.

Finally, I'll abruptly end this brief essay with … first … no hint of who I think the killer was, because I haven't the slightest clue. And second … with the unabashed claim that if DNA and modern forensic science had been available back then, the mystery would have been cracked in short order.

But just imagine, if that had been the case, we probably wouldn't have such a lasting melodrama, would we?

"Now I'll end with humor, which I didn't do last time. It's a comedic routine I've borrowed from George Carlin and it isn't dirty, I assure you. I call it, *Ode to Life's Little Stages*.

"Do you realize that the only time in our lives when we like to get old is when we're kids? If you're less than 10 years old, you're so excited about aging that you think in fractions.

"How old are you?"

"I'm four and a half!" Later on, you're never thirty-six and a half. But now, you're four and a half.

"You get into your teens, and now they can't hold you back You jump to the next number, or even a few ahead.

"How old are you?"

"I'm gonna be 16!" You could be 13, but hey, you're gonna be 16!

"And then, the greatest day of your life. You BECOME 21. Even the words sound like a ceremony. YOU BECOME 21.

"Next, you turn 30. Oooohh, what happened there? Makes you sound like bad milk. He TURNED. We had to throw him out. There's no fun now. He's just a sour-dumpling. What's wrong? What's changed?

"You BECOME 21; you TURN 30 … then you're PUSHING 40. Whoa! Put on the brakes. It's all slipping away. And before you know it, you REACH 50. Your dreams are gone.

"But wait! You MAKE it to 60. Maybe you didn't think you would!

"So you BECOME 21, TURN 30, PUSH 40, REACH 50 and MAKE it to 60.

"You've built up so much speed that you HIT 70.

"After that, it's a day-by-day thing: you HIT Wednesday!

"You get into your 80s and every day is a complete cycle: you HIT lunch; you TURN 4:30; you reach BEDTIME.

And it doesn't end there. Into the 90s, you start going backwards: "I was JUST 92."

"Then a strange thing happens. If you make it to over 100, you become a little kid again: "I'm 100 and a half!"

"May you all make it to a healthy 100 and a half!"

There was more laughing than clapping. During it, a man jumped up and hollered "hallelulia". Rick was tempted to reach for his .45 until he recognized him as one of the laundry workers.

He then motioned Foster aside and said, "Now it's time to look into the money problem here. First off, have you heard from your counterparts in any other hospitals?"

"Not at all. And I haven't inquired. Not yet anyway."

"Well don't. I'll handle it. I've thought of Yale. The administrator there is Jay Dietrick who was a Yale classmate of mine and we've remained close. I'll call him and I'm sure he'll share information with me on the phone, especially if I tell him what's happening with us. Meanwhile, how'd you find out about what's going on here? I mean money-wise."

As a good portion of the audience was thinning out, Foster grabbed Rick's hand and led him into an empty side pantry. There they sat side by side and Foster removed some crumpled up notes from his breast pocket.

"What would I do without notes?" he asked. He straightened them out and continued: "For years, I've received monthly reports from the front office about what various insurance companies have sent us as payments for services rendered here. It's a figure that represents the combined amount from all of them, and I'm talking about thousands. A thousand or so either way. I would study the forms pretty thoroughly. And then I got sloppy, because I simply began glancing at them. Well, Rick, you guessed it. Starting just four months ago, even only a glance showed that there was a sudden drop in the amount. I'd say 20 per cent. So, that's when …"

"Hold on, Terry. I've heard enough. Let's see if the percentage and the timing match elsewhere. As I said, I'll start with good old Yale."

Chapter 10

Rick had called Fran, outlining all that had occurred since they departed Romania, and asking if he'd join him at the Hole. Fran did, arriving there from his nearby Stamford home within the hour.

He dropped into one of the three chairs there, with Rick taking the next one and balancing his stuffed satchel on the other.

Fran looked around. "Quite a place you have here," he said. "Is a vent called a 'hole within a Hole?'"

"Ha-ha," Rick said. "Let's get serious. You're my alter-ego, you know."

"And you're mine. So we have two alter-egos. Do they gang up on either of us?"

"Probably me," Rick said

"Rather it be me," Fran said. "I'm just along for the ride."

Rick raised up, put his arm around him and commented, "You're more than that, my friend."

They both stared at one another in silence until Fran broke it: "So what's on the docket?"

"Well, I think I brought you up to date on the important things, but let's investigate them one at a time. The business of our hospital getting less money than usual heads that list."

"No," Fran interrupted. "Heading the overall list is the

threats you've gotten. And *then* it's the money question."

Rick's response was delivered in a wry but reflex manner: "Correct, but I said 'investigate', not 'worry about'. I don't even know where to begin with the threats. But for now, the best we can do is to be well prepared and to wait and see what develops. You agree?"

"You've clarified it. Yes."

"Okay then. So I'd like to find out if other hospitals are having the same problem and, after some lunch, I'd like to start with Yale. You know how many beds they have there?"

"Certainly more than here."

"I'll say. I downloaded 'Yale New Haven Hospital'. They currently have twice as many beds as we do … 1,540. Meaning if they're being victimized too, then the amount should be twice as much as here. Unless the perps don't figure it that way"

Chapter 11

Their lunch was consumed in record time. Then Rick phoned Yale and had no difficulty getting through to Jay Dietrick.

Rick's simple "Afternoon, Jay", was followed by no preliminary remarks as he went directly to the reason for the call. "I have a question for you," he said.

"Wait, Rick, I know what you're going to ask. I was about to call you myself. The answer is yes. We're getting snookered. Just like Hollings. Right?"

"Right. How much there?"

"Not sure yet. Our accounting office is working on it … checking, double-checking; waiting themselves for an accurate figure. They're also getting some kind of a hint that a single insurance company might be behind it all."

"And holding on to a percentage for its own personal use?"

"Or diverting it somewhere for money laundering."

"Could be that or other criminal reasons. You think the amount that's kept could be 20 %?"

"At least."

"You know of any other hospitals with the same problem?"

"No, but I'll make some calls. Maybe Danbury, Bridgeport and Middletown. So I'll let you know."

The conversation, brief but revealing — almost stinging — left Rick wondering what his next move should be, aside from filling Fran in with

Dietrick's words. Then Rick wandered back to his talk with David, when he professed that he wouldn't be caught off-guard if the immediate future contained more travel. And possibly international in scope.

"You'd be ready for that?" he asked Fran.

"Ready."

"And you'd be with me?"

"Of course."

"Thank you … and thank you, Lord."

The phone rang and Rick picked up the receiver as leisurely as he could stage it. It was Lance who said he'd already checked with his histarians. They had learned about the "withholding issue", as they phrased it, and the fact that the hospitals were not withholding the monies for their own personal use. Also that the leader or leaders of the operation were most likely not hospital personnel. But they hadn't yet discovered the exact hospitals involved. On the positive side, however, the histarians had provided him with two relevant lists. Number one was about receipt money somehow being earmarked for four things: money laundering, kickbacks, organized crime, and cybercrime. And number two was that the participating countries were Ireland, Italy and Greece. For Ireland, they sited Dublin. In Italy, it was Rome; and in Greece, it was Athens. They also indicated that they knew how important sightseeing was in Rick's travels, so they suggested he start Ireland in Killarney.

As he was listening to what Lance was saying, Rick was scribbling as fast as he could onto a scratch pad.

"Is that enough for now?" Lance asked.

Rick's "whew" did little to answer the question, much less to limit the sweat he felt at the back of his neck. The usual place. He could almost hear it developing.

"Good job," Rick said, "and I appreciate it. A lot on my plate and it might take me some time to figure it all out. But let's keep each other informed."

He then flipped through his pad and, as best he could, informed Fran of what Lance had said. After that, Rick went for a towel, wiped his neck, and then sat to think. It didn't take much time for him to realize that his mind had become more crowded than ever. And it was the lists of crimes and countries that had done it. However, the funneling of hospital receipts into organized crime activity, kickbacks, and cybercrime functions **had** to be addressed, as did visits to the three countries. He thought it ironic that he had once before worked with the police departments in Dublin, Rome and Athens on separate occasions and considered each one a stimulating experience — and a successful one.

Yet, what else to do? What else to do?

There was no one instructing him about a time constraint, so the decision was his, and his alone. Yet before that were thoughts that pushed all others aside. He rammed them through his mind, one after the other, and soon a single one rose above them all: "I need a break. A change of pace. What better kind than to conduct my usual judo class at Bruno's tomorrow morning, a Thursday. I've skipped them for two straight weeks.And Fran? He can relax in the waiting room for the hour. Unless he wants to take my class!"

Chapter 12

In Hartford, they arrived at the parking lot of the old stucco building that housed Bruno's Martial Arts Studio at just before nine and edged their way along a winding path to the front entrance. Rick brought along his over-stacked satchel which, in view of recent developments, he had rummaged through earlier to be certain it contained all he wanted it to contain. In it, besides inches and inches of papers and folders, were several rounds of ammunition, a pair of binoculars, a postage stamp-sized digital tape recorder, a Taser, a small container of Mace tear gas spray, a policeman's whistle, a scout knife, a box of latex surgical gloves, a tactical flashlight, and an extra cell phone. He put the Mace in his pocket, thinking he'd take it along wherever he went.

From a dishwater sky, an incessant fall rain drizzled on. The air smelled swampy and the sounds were natural enough — recurring gusts from afar, the snap and swish of branches behind them, drips from sloping eaves. The rain itself was now silent. Rick felt on edge.

One again he cursed the three flights of stairs he had to climb. And he hated the upcoming routine at his locker where he changed into a pajama-like costume of a black-bordered white cotton jacket and pants, even though he'd done so for 15 years. But he always enjoyed his black belt status; the class he conducted; and the ensuing routine of refining his own skills in percussive *tae kwan do* combat with fellow instructors: kicking, elbowing, slashing with hands and feet. They all knew how to be gentle with one another, their body parts stopping just short of contact.

Rick opened the door at the top of the stairs, its laminated glass panel bearing the words:

CHINESE, JAPANESE, KOREAN, AMERICAN
MARTIAL ARTS
BRUNO BATEMAN, GRAND MASTER

Unlike ever before, Rick had a strong premonition that his competency in karate would serve him well in the next few weeks. Especially the *bujutsu* phase that stresses not only combat but also a willingness to face death as a matter of honor. Such was the respect he'd developed for the spiritual concepts it's based on: Zen Buddhism and Shinto.

He noticed Bruno beginning a class in a side room and waved to him.

The Grand Master interrupted his instruction and stepped out to greet Rick and to be introduced to Fran.

He then shook Rick's hand again and said, "I see by your papers that the hospital's still receiving many requests for help. What a place! Well, you can continue to postpone your work here whenever you have to."

Rick smiled and reached out to squeeze Bruno's hand and wrist with his right and left hands, but he was unable to make the Grand Master bend his knees.

He was nearly as tall as Rick but much thinner, all muscle and no fat. In his sixties, he had run the studio for half his life and once confided to Rick that if it were not for karate, he would have gone into medicine.

"But really," he qualified, "I would never have made it into medical school."

"Sure you would, except for that ponytail of yours."

Rick regarded him steadily. "You didn't have it back then, did you?"

"Of course. It's the seat of my power."

With Fran relaxing among magazines in the waiting room, Rick began his class, recapturing the sensations that were spawned on most Thursday mornings: the smell of sweat, the faint talcum taste, the give of the shiaijo mat under his bare feet.

An hour later, he took a quick shower, signaled Fran, and they left. They made their way to the parking lot and although the soft ground was absorbing Rick's footprints, the rain had totally stopped. Bits of gray sky showed high above, as gray as something else that entered his stream of thought: would there be a threatening note on his car? It had happened once before and he was ready for it to happen again. He approached the Mercedes slowly, casting an eye in every direction.

Then out of nowhere, two short men appeared directly in front of Rick, guns pointing at his head. The men wore black masks.

Fran reached for his own gun.

"No, don't!" Rick shrieked as he executed what had taken him four years to master, right there at Bruno's. Known as the BKM or bilateral karate maneuver, it was a chop using both hands simultaneously against two opponent's arms and, at the same time, launching a leg sweep at each of them. Rick executed the maneuver with swiftness and dexterity and, in the process, had to fall to the ground. But he arose without injury.

Meanwhile the men plummeted down heavily and while they were groaning, Rick patted them down and found large rolls of American dollars in each one's pants pocket. Then Rick pulled off their masks. Their faces gave little hint of origin except possibly Oriental.

Suddenly one man rolled over and tried to recover his gun, but Fran stomped on his hand. Then the men were hoisted to their feet and, at that point, Rick rattled off a series of questions: Were you being paid to kill me? Who sent you here? Does Dracula mean anything to you?

Receiving no response, they were dragged into the Studio where Rick asked Bruno to stop his teaching and hear what had just transpired. After that, the assailants were roped to a pole and the Grand Master gave assurance that he would notify the police. He said it as if he would do so after his class was over. But Rick, his sweat having returned, said they would wait until the police arrived.

He was elated that he had full command of the situation but couldn't help wondering how the masked men knew of his destination and precisely when he'd arrive there. *Or was I a mistake? Did they pick on the wrong guy?* He asked Fran about it and received only a shrug of his shoulders.

The elation was combined with appreciation directed at long-time friend, Paul D'Arneau … for convincing him to join Bruno's as an eventual instructor. After earning his black belt, he had been given the responsibility of teaching students how to fall safely and how to strengthen the muscles used in judo. He then helped the students acquire skills involving a foot sweep, hip throw, rear throw, shoulder throw, and various hand chops.

And now, while sitting impatiently on a side bench, Rick felt that being the wrong person under attack was unlikely. If so, however, he was still left with why, where and when.

Since it hadn't been the first time that assailants had faced him, and since the police had arrived and hauled them away, Rick was able to put this episode aside, for he had grown weary of them. Even hardened.

He'd also grown weary of memories that dealt with the Balkans and even with hospital financial receipts. He said to Fran, "The Balkans deserve the memories. The hospital disasters do not."

What had now become "center stage" was the number of phone calls to Hollings General — ones that dealt with problems among the general public — "Counsel Calls". He understood that the number had increased dramatically, but he hadn't personally followed through with any of them yet.

All of this was the kind of thinking his mind was accustomed to over the years when, say, three problems were at hand but his mind figured it was double that number. And he understood such a propensity, often tried to rationalize it away, but was seldom successful. So, for the time being at least, he would try his best to restrict his thinking to: checking with three countries about four types of crime, and dealing with the public's non-medical concerns. He believed the restriction had some semblance of a proper *modus operandi.* And Fran agreed.

Also, they both felt that checking with the countries should not be done by phone — only in person. That phone calls have a certain limitation, in and of itself. Not so with the in-person approach and the value of body language.

Chapter 13

Returning to the hospital — Fran at his side — Rick checked with the front office about calls that had been received from individuals asking for help. There were many of them and he decided to appoint a committee of four administrative assistants to handle these and future ones with the option of seeking his advice whenever necessary. He labeled all such calls as "Counsel Calls". And he asked one assistant to act as the hospital's top security official if he, Rick, were away while handling a caller's request.

But as of then, one stood out above all the others. It was made by the wife of Dr. Mark Kralin, a practicing physician and consultant to the U.N. A telegram had arrived at their New York City home warning them about an explosion that would occur at the nearby United Nations General Assembly Building. It didn't say why or when but indicated that another telegram would explain it all within 24 hours.

A series of explosions had taken place there three years before, and Rick remembered reading about them in a novel titled, *Disaster and More*. It was written by an author who used the incidents to embellish his thoughts on biofeedback and transcendental meditation.

In her call, Mrs. Kralin had left their phone number and simply asked about what to do besides informing the police. Rick phoned her and said that they should alert the U.N. Security Force right now and wait for the second telegram to arrive. If such a telegram were to be more explicit and positive about an explosion, the Force would immediately be expanded and it would handle the situation as a dire emergency.

He also informed her of the novel and said that he didn't know if the main character in it was the same person who had sent the telegram.

"It's a possibility," he said, "but at this stage, who's to know?" He added that the book was in his home and he could hardly wait to reread parts of it. "Perhaps," he said, "there's much in it that might help us now."

Rick had no trouble finding the book among the stacks in his study and he leafed through it until he found the chapter about the U.N. explosions. He then began reading it, handing over every page to Fran for him to read also. Rick often paused to determine if anything applied to the Kralin case. From Chapter 18 on, they read:

> Luis Rivera had been working at the United Nations since his arrival in the States. Although they had not married, he and Laura lived together in her beautifully kept, small brick Tudor within walking distance of Cornell Medical Center. He didn't mind the hour-and-a-half commute along the Merritt Parkway to the majestic building complex bordering New York's East River, listening to music or "how to" tapes or catching up on dictation and, on his return trip, generally decompressing. He had rented a two-room apartment in the city for use when things ran late, usually once or twice a week.
>
> He began as one of a host of Spanish interpreters in the General Assembly but soon became part of Mexico's diplomatic mission, rising from a junior attaché to a Counselor in less than a year. Then, because of his extensive satellite and communication background, he was appointed consultant to the International Communications Union, a specialized U.N. agency helping nations solve problems in radio, telephone, telegraph and satellite communications. The Union's principal headquarters were in Geneva, Switzerland.
>
> He and Laura were having an infrequent, quiet Saturday dinner at home. The quaint dining room was surrounded on three sides by window seats beneath tall windows, one of which looked

on to a round flower garden encircling a flagpole. The lawn was too small to be considered "grounds" but too large for two people to maintain, especially when one was employed 80 miles away or, sometimes four thousand. "Cricket Lawn and Garden Service" served them well.

It was early spring in New England. Not a single day passed when Luis didn't call attention to the fragrance and loveliness of Laura's red and pink roses that brightened a split rail fence running the length of the driveway.

"It's funny, Laura," he said one evening, "I live a little bit in New York but my main home is in Connecticut. And I have a little headquarters in New York, but my main headquarters are in Geneva. I'm like a satellite in living and working."

"You're so clever, my love," she said adoringly.

"More loving than clever."

She savored those words for a few seconds, then said, "Luis, will you promise me something?"

"Yes, I promise. For you, anything."

"Don't ever change."

"But I couldn't ever change until I die."

Laura was not completely sure what that meant but convinced herself it didn't matter. And she was not sure about something else, something that had been bothering her. Now was as good a time as any, so she plunged right into it.

"What is it about storms?" she asked.

"Storms? Well, you see, I like both Nature's calm and her fury."

"Enough to dash out into thunder and lightning?"

"But one is safe in a car in weather like that."

"That's not the point, dear. Why go out in the first place?"

"Because the fury won't come to me."

"Let's hope not," she said.

For well over a year, she watched him monitor weather patterns in North America with the fervor of a stockbroker following market fluctuations. Working his computer, he had kept up a special interest in Mexican weather: its air masses, winds, pressures and cloudbursts; its cyclone and anti-cyclone phenomena.

Laura couldn't figure it out. "It's like some kind of hobby since you were a kid, I suppose."

"Yes. That's it. Since I was a kid. It's a hobby to keep me out of trouble."

"But not off wet streets."

They both chuckled.

On a Monday, Dr. Mark Kralin was in New York attending a medical conference at Cornell Medical Center and had some free time after two early morning lectures. He thought he would chance it and phoned Laura who gave him Luis' number at the U.N. She also confirmed that he was there and not in Geneva.

Luis sounded euphoric on the phone. Mark asked about having lunch and they agreed to meet at a restaurant, familiar to both, near the medical center.

There was a method to Mark's call for lunch: he had heard that Luis had just finished writing a yet unpublished book on satellite capabilities, and wanted to inquire about any ramifications regarding the improvement of medical cooperation among nations.

Mark was the first to arrive and was seated at a table sipping a Diet Sprite when a smiling Luis bounced in. The popular restaurant was packed and noisy, a lunchtime environment they were both used to.

"Obviously I reached you on a happy day," Mark said.

"I'm most happy, Mark, for I've just this morning learned that my book will be published."

"Marvelous, Luis! Congratulations. I heard about it, and I think that's absolutely — well — wonderful." In celebration, Mark switched his drink to a Bloody Mary and Luis joined him.

He explained that he'd been working on the manuscript for four years and he was probably the first Mexican to have worked in that field.

"Tell me about it," Mark said, careful to nurse his drink since there was still a long afternoon of medical discussions ahead at the Center.

"I'll never forget, my friend, when I met you and your fine family at Christmas time and I overdid the explanation of my work. I won't make the same mistake now."

"Before you start though, what's the title of the book?"

"Earth Observation Satellites."

"Sounds intriguing," Mark said. "Makes you wonder what they can observe."

"Good point. Excellent point. I hope potential readers feel that way."

There was a brief lull before Luis proceeded: Well, earth observation satellites are used to monitor our planet's resources with guess what?"

Mark shook his head.

"Photographs. There are lots and lots in the book. Then computers on earth analyze the pictures in a first go-around. They can rapidly weed out the informative ones and cancel out those that would contribute little. In the second go-around, scientists get their chance to analyze and are able to determine many things, like identifying sources of pollution or locating mineral deposits or detecting the spread of disease."

"Aha!" Mark exclaimed.

"I mean disease in crops and forests."

Mark, thinking out loud, said, "But couldn't some of this apply to the spread of human disease? I'm not sure how, but maybe by implication or something?"

"You bring up a good point and as a matter of fact, I have two chapters devoted to just that. At this point it's all theoretical, but I do discuss exactly what you're suggesting. And I take a big leap in predicting that the study of disease spread — human, farm-related, whatever — will someday have a bearing on shared scientific knowledge among all countries. It's because of greater world travel, greater tourism. The globe is smaller now. I even spend time on new discoveries scientists have not yet shared on the international level. In areas like institutional conditioning or in medicine per se."

Mark could hardly believe what he had just heard. It was as though there had been some telepathic link between them, one that had prompted him to place an impromptu call to Luis in the first place. He was nearing the end of his drink and beginning to feel its effects. Luis, having done most of the talking, had barely touched his.

"Could you come and speak to our county medical society one of these days?" Mark asked.

"It would be my pleasure. And if I could help someone, I would be honored."

Luis tossed off the bulk of his drink and they devoured the stiffening hamburgers they had let sit during their discussion.

In the parking lot, as they were about to go their separate ways, with the new author still beaming over the earlier good news and with Mark happy for him, Mark said, "Biofeedback, transcendental meditation. Fantastic stuff."

The following Monday, disaster struck, as a series of explosions shocked the country and the world. They occurred in the auditorium of the United Nations General Assembly Building, the Delegates Lounge of the Conference Building, and on the great tapestried staircase of the Secretariat — like the surgical strikes of the Gulf War.

Mark heard the news bulletin on his car radio, listening in the parking lot of the Medical Center, turning up the volume, biting his lip. Once inside, he sat glued to the T.V. in the doctors' lounge and by noon had called Laura to ask about Luis' safety. She wasn't able to reach him. He moved into his office to review the details of the calamity alone and to mull over what he had learned from her.

There had been one brief concussion and six simultaneous low-volume blasts before it was over. It lasted only a few seconds. There was no fire. Structural damage was minimal but thick smoke and flying debris were deadly. No outer walls were affected nor any major interior contents such as the impressive semi-circular table in the Security Council Chamber, the spectacular structures in the General Assembly Building, or the artificial satellite in its lobby.

Nothing on the grounds had been disturbed. The statue representing peace and called, "Let Us Beat Swords Into Plowshares", was still standing.

The ambassadors and chargé d'affaires of Libya, Iraq, Iran, North Korea, North Vietnam and Cuba were killed instantly.

That was it: quick, precise, all in a neat package. Twelve diplomats wiped out in a flash. There was none of the widespread devastation like that of the World Trade Center or the Oklahoma City bombings, but reaction around the globe was much swifter, more intense and unexpected. The consensus was that people everywhere — accustomed to suspicious plane crashes and massive public explosions in the Middle East, London, Northern Ireland, Paris, Bosnia-Herzegovina and the United States — would have been less terrified had one giant blast rocked the United Nations. But psychologically, the notion of isolated, synchronized blasts like this, implied a greater sophistication of terrorist activity. Six individualized but simultaneous explosions had occurred. Had terrorism come this far?

But even beyond that, it was the location of the attack that hit home the hardest. The United Nations. The Symbol of World Peace. That is where they labored to prevent things like this from happening elsewhere. Nearly every nation on the face of the globe was represented at that place which provided a collective security. Bettering mankind. What next?

Repercussions from the Orson Welles *War of the Worlds* were nothing compared to the panic that set in on that early Monday morning. Airborne aircraft of the United States Strategic Air Command tripled. Nuclear subs went on red alert. Countries braced en masse, recalling military personnel on leave, revving up artillery hardware and bolstering border patrols. Politicians took to the airwaves to reassure constituents. The United States president went on television. And some New York Prophets of

Armageddon dropped everything and flocked toward "safer ground" in upper New England.

"Are you all right?" Laura screamed into the phone. She had been trying for hours to reach Luis at the U.N. and finally, with the help of the central dispatch office of her department's Communications Center, contact was made. She was told by a telephone operator that because of the flood of calls, she and her respondent were allowed only 30 seconds on line.

"Yes, yes, don't worry," Luis said. "I was nowhere near the trouble. I'll be staying overnight to help out."

"Okay, but please keep me posted, darling. Thank God! Be careful. And oh …" she remembered to comment, "T.V. says the dozen who died were our enemies."

"That's correct. Not the people though, just the governments."

"Strange, isn't it?" she asked. I mean just those specific countries."

"Not if someone wanted it to be. I must go, my love. I'll call you at home tonight."

The frenzy of the aftermath had never been seen before. FBI, CIA, ATF, bomb squads, local law enforcement personnel, the media, politicians, foreign government officials, and police dogs — all were scouring the area within minutes. Assured that the structures were safe, the U.N. Security Council met in emergency session. Security was increased at all terminals. All day on television, the number of news interruptions was so great that networks decided to cancel their regularly scheduled programming in order to offer up-to-the-minute coverage of "the most bizarre calamity ever recorded". A sense of imminent doom blanketed the globe.

> One major newspaper released an early edition with the following summary: “Twelve high-level government officials from six distinct countries were killed. Six individual flashing blasts tore twelve isolated, clearly demarcated holes in the fabric of world peace and safety”.
>
> Shock waves reverberated for weeks and the investigation never ended. Even Luis was interrogated at length about his exact whereabouts at the time of the incident, his immediate reaction to it, and his current plans as a result of it. His answers to these three queries were:
>
> “In the men’s room.”
>
> “Shock and horror.”
>
> “Continuing my service in the search for a lasting peace.”

– – –

During their reading, there was no attempt on the part of either Rick or Fran to bypass any of the words. For a moment, Rick thought “terrorism” might have had some relevance, but aside from relating it to his recent terrorism reading in Belgrade, he dismissed the thought.

All told, he was more captivated by what he had just read than he was in Belgrade, but reasoned that one reading was for pleasure while this one was for information purposes. Information he never found.

Then shortly before Luis was about to leave for Geneva, the second telegram arrived. It read: “Sorry. Just kidding. No explosion. But I bet I awoke the sleeping giants there. Or are they dwarfs?”

PART TWO

Chapter 14

Since the circulation of the Hollings newspaper had tripled, the number of calls had increased nearly as much. Some came from people Rick termed "sound as a dollar". Others he termed "sound as a jerko". And in the case of the two telegrams and the time spent reading about nothing that ever even happened, he was deeply disturbed over the entire episode's being staged by just such a person — a very *sick* jerko. The reading about Luis and Laura had especially registered as an entire waste of time, and Rick was cocksure that the jerko was not the same person who had written the book he had bothered to read. So because of total dismay, Rick didn't rush to solve the problems of other callers. In fact, he decided to forsake any more local requests and to turn his attention to Dublin, Rome and Athens. Even more foreign countries than that, if necessary.

He was in the Hole at the time and Fran was there with him. They were discussing the business of time spent in Europe at the expense of time devoted to more local issues. Out of it came some interrelated approaches suggested by Rick and frowned upon by Fran. Rick had been making notes on his pad — adding, crossing out, underlining. Eventually, he took time to write out things more clearly and completely after which he looked up at Fran and said that a series of approaches should include:

One — Their reading about each particular country or region ahead of arrival there. Rick said he'd already boned up on Ireland.

Two — Prompting important European initiatives by making the same reading source available to key foreign leaders. That Joe Gomez might help in identifying them.

Three — Honoring the information that histarian Lance Beck had provided: Visit Ireland, Italy and Greece. And address money laundering, kickbacks, organized crime, and cybercrime.

"Now Fran, my good buddy, I saw your frown. You question why and I question why not?"

"But a single article can't capture everything important," Fran responded.

"No, but it's not a simple article I have in mind. It's longer than that … a piece I found in the *National Geographic.* And it begins the process. Sets the tone. So let's go with it in Ireland. If it proves worthwhile, we continue that way. If it doesn't, we stop it."

With that, he handed Fran a map of Europe with writing that began on its top side. "Here," he said, pointing to the words. "Do read it now. I've only skimmed over what it says, but I made a copy of it, and I'll be reading it more thoroughly now, just like you are. Agreed?"

"Agreed, my good buddy."

"And I don't know whether you realize it or not, Fran, but while in Europe we'll get to do more sightseeing."

Rick frowned again, and then they began reading:

> As of now, June, 2005, and through a purely geographic lens, Europe ambles from Iceland to Greece to Russia's Ural Mountains, with Moscow well within its bounds. But at its soul, Europe is more a concept than a continent. A political idea increasingly shaped by the European Union. Today that partnership embraces landscapes and cultures that are more disparate than at any time in history. The EU's motto: *in varietate concordia*, united in diversity.
>
> In May 2004, the EU admitted ten countries, including eight former communist countries, a historic expansion that formed a

> 25-member bloc with 457 million people. Several more countries are clamoring to join. The appeal? As part of a single-market economy, EU members tend to gain wealth, stability, and political clout. But rapid expansion has raised tensions over ethnic, religious, and cultural identity, leading some to fear that more growth will dilute the EU's newfound strength. And the idea of Europe itself.
>
> The titans of European history, from Charlemagne to Napoleon, fought to unite Europe by the sword and the gun. Not until after the horrors of World War II did leaders try to unify the continent without bloodshed. Hoping to secure peac by linking their economies and governments, Western European leaders in 1951 created the precursor to today's European Union. What started as a small, six-nation alliance has grown, with its enlargement last year, to include almost all of western and central Europe. "The first of May 2004 will go down in history as the day of the continent's unification, when Europe's decades-long divide was healed; when a dream was realized" declared then European Commission President Romano Prodi in a speech after the unprecedented expansion.
>
> Now a sprawling conglomerate, the EU operates in 20 official languages and includes some of the world's most affluent cities as well as impoverished rural pockets. Switzerland, Norway and Iceland have not joined; Romania, Bulgaria and Croatia are expected to enter in a few years, and Turkey officially begins membership negotiations this fall.

"I just don't know," Rick said, folding his copy and sliding it into his satchel.

"You just don't know what?" Fran asked.

"Certain countries not joining; certain ones possibly backing off. Who's to say? And with such vast divides in resources and cultures, one question seems to predominate: What does it mean to be European? Go figure."

Chapter 15

Rick didn't waste any time. He met with Foster and asked for a two-week leave of absence. He had never told the administrator about the threat he'd received plus the encounter at Bruno's Studio, and now was the perfect time to do so. He told of the rock thrown through his window with the paper wrapped around it. And also of the two gun-toting men he had to level to the ground.

"I'm choosing not to go into detail about my absence" he said, "but I need to accomplish some things in a few countries that are dealing with the problem we're having over receipt money. Beginning with Ireland. But I'll be back. In the meantime, if there's anything you have to share with me before that, do call my wife Angela. I'll be checking with her on a regular basis."

It was a meeting he believed might have led to some friction, but it didn't. On the contrary. Foster seemed to measure Rick's request with his own sloppiness concerning the hospital's receipts.

"And if we get done sooner than in two weeks, I'll see you sooner," Rick said. "I say 'we' because my friend Fran will be with me."

He left Foster's office having covered all that he wished to cover and was astonished that Foster hadn't asked for an elaboration of the European trip.

Back at the Hole, Rick gathered up some things — papers, maps, writing materials — and stuffed them into his satchel. For the first time ever, he complained of the dwindling space in it.

Fran had arrived earlier and now watched and finally said, "You know, I might get you a bigger one, come Christmas."

“Thanks but don’t you dare. I’d have to unload this one, and no telling what I’d find. The worst would be anything reminding me of the Balkans. For now, let’s just concentrate on countries, crimes and what else?” Rick included the last three words, not as something he’d forgotten but as a legitimate question.

“Let’s see,” Fran said, “I’d say it’s a toss-up between Rome’s Colosseum and Greece’s Parthenon.”

“So sightseeing comes in third?”

“Oh, I forgot about that one!”

Rick faked a karate chop and they both laughed.

“Seriously though,”Rick said, “You’re well aware of my sightseeing obsession.”

“Oh yes. I like some of it myself. Also, I don’t think it’s an obsession, but I do know you like to have *Vérité’s* Leon Cassel and Ansel Stewart in our travels. I could give them a call.”

“Excellent,” Rick said. “Tell them we’ll be starting in Ireland, and leave the rest to me. Oh, and where do we meet them? Make it the Yale library. You figure out the time. Then we can all leave for Europe together. But getting back to the sightseeing, you won’t get disgusted if I ask for more, will you? You have in the past. It’s your silence that gets to me.”

“No, I wouldn’t be disgusted.”

Their give and take reminded Rick of two squirrels taking bites from the same nut. But he enjoyed it.

Fran left for his home and Rick heard back from him about an hour later. “Both Leon and Ansel said they’d very much like to accompany us, now and on future missions. So there. You’ll have your triad with you wherever. They’ll be at the library tomorrow morning at nine, our time.”

After that call, Rick placed one to Chief Gomez and brought him up to date. "I need your help again," Rick said. "Fran, Leon, Ansel and I are about to fly to Europe, not the Balkan countries, but to three others: Ireland, Italy and Greece. We need to communicate with some police or other government officials. I've worked with one in Ireland before, in Dublin. But for the other two, only in passing . You know any in Rome or Athens?"

"In both. Very well, in fact. They've come down here to Buenos Aires a couple of times for an international seminar, and I've gone there for the same thing. One's Cesare Ciccone. The other is Mike Kotsos. Both police captains. You want me to contact them? Then when you get there, you can just go to their central office right in the middle of the city."

"How about in Dublin?" Rick asked.

"Yeah, there too. Nice young captain named Ronnie O'Brien."

"Oh yes, I remember him. Easy to work with. Could you call him too?"

"Certainly. That way, you'll have all three expecting you."

"Perfect," Rick said. "It's 'laying the groundwork'. And I should explain. What we have to talk about is too complicated to begin covering over the phone. Just say it will all keep and that we're anxious to meet them. We'll start in Ireland. Killarney first, for a little sightseeing before Dublin."

Rick paused to rethink what he had just said, and then continued. "And Joe? I'm not being too bossy with you, am I?"

Gomez then paused himself before answering. "No, you never have and you aren't now."

Before retiring for the night, Rick ran through the upper level of a side book rack to locate a book containing extensive accounts of well-known crimes. Taken from *Wikipedia*, it included the four on the list provided by Lance. But ever the one to be totally prepared, he read through them and then typed out synopses. His intent was to have a compendium of facts, should anything slip his mind in Europe. And as an offshoot of this, perhaps some clues as to how to proceed might take form. What he extracted was the following:

—Money laundering: the illegal process of concealing the origins of money obtained by passing it through a complex sequence of banking transfers or commercial transactions. The overall scheme of this process returns the money to the launderer in an obscure and indirect way.

One problem of criminal activities is accounting for the proceeds without raising suspicion of law enforcement agencies. Considerable time and effort may be put into strategies which enable the safe use of those proceeds without raising unwanted suspicion. Implementing such strategies is generally called money laundering. After money has been laundered, it can be used for legitimate purposes.

Law enforcement agencies of many jurisdictions have set up sophisticated systems in an effort to detect suspicious transactions or activities, and many have set up cooperative international arrangements to assist each other in these endeavors.

In a number of legal and regulatory systems, the term "money laundering" has become conflated with other forms of financial and business crime, and is sometimes used more generally to include misuse of the financial system (including things such as securities, digital currencies, credit cards, and traditional currency) and evasion of international sanctions.

—Cybercrime or Computer-oriented Crime. This is one that involves a computer and a network. The computer may have been used in the commission of a crime, or it may be the target. Cybercrimes can be defined as offenses that are committed against individuals or a group of individuals with a criminal motive to intentionally harm the reputation of the victim, or cause physical or mental harm, or loss, to the victim directly or indirectly, using modern telecommunication networks such as Internet and mobile phones. Cybercrime may threaten a person or a nation's security and financial health. Issues surrounding these types of crime have become high-profile, particularly those surrounding hacking, copyright infringement, unwarranted mass-surveillance, sextortion, child pornography, and child grooming. There are also problems of privacy when confidential information is intercepted or disclosed, lawfully or otherwise.

—Kickback (Bribery). A kickback is a form of negotiated bribery in which a commission is paid to the bribe-taker in exchange for services rendered. Generally speaking, the remuneration (money, goods, or services handed over) is negotiated ahead of time. The kickback varies from other kinds of bribes in that there is implied collusion between agents of the two parties, rather than one party extorting the bribe from the other. The purpose of the kickback is usually to encourage the other party to cooperate in the illegal scheme.

The term "kickback" comes from colloquial English language, and describes the way a recipient of illegal gain "kicks back" a portion of it to another person for that person's assistance in obtaining it.

The most common form of kickback involves a vendor submitting a fraudulent or inflated invoice (often for goods or services which were not needed, of inferior quality, or both) with an employee of the victim company assisting in securing payment. For his or her assistance in securing payment, the individual receives some sort of payment (cash, goods, services) or favor (the hiring of a relative, employment, etc.)

"Kickback brokers" are individuals who may not receive the kickback personally, but who help link the individual or company providing the goods or services with individuals capable of assisting with the illegal payments. For helping to link the two colluding parties, either or both parties may make a payment to this "broker".

—Organized crime. This is a category of transnational, national, or local groupings of highly centralized enterprises run by criminals who intend to engage in illegal activity, most commonly for profit. Some criminal organizations, such as terrorist groups, are politically motivated. Sometimes criminal organizations force people to do business with them, such as when a gang extorts money from shopkeepers for "protection". Gangs may become disciplined enough to be considered *organized.* A *criminal organization* or gang can also be referred to as a *mafia, ring, or syndicate*; the network, subculture and community of criminals may be referred to as the *underworld.*

Other organizations including states, churches, militaries, police forces, and corporations may sometimes use organized crime methods to conduct their activities, but their power derives from their status as formal social institutions. There is a tendency to distinguish organized crime from other forms of crime, such as white-collar crime, financial crimes, political crimes, war crime, state crimes, and treason. This distinction is not always apparent and academics continue to debate the matter. For example, in failed states that can no longer perform basic functions such as education, security, or governance (usually due to fractious violence or to extreme poverty) organized crime, governance and war sometimes complement each other. The term "oligarchy" has been used to describe democratic countries whose political, social and economic institutions come under the control of a few families and business oligarchs.

He then slithered the four synopses into his satchel.

Chapter 16

They landed at Kerry Airport and just after disembarking, Rick said, "I suggest we sightsee during the mornings and then, after lunch, we go to work. And I'm not insisting we sightsee near and far. Near would be fine with me. It's like I'd be taking a pill, not a bunch of them. After all, we're here on a mission. In fact, I've decided to modify the sightseeing idea: if there are places we can't see in person, we can read about them in the many posters we're sure to come across. So, as Lance learned from the histarians, it's Killarney and Dublin. The first for what? Sightseeing, of course.

"Now we need an overall plan. Remember what's been going on? Hospital receipt money is being funneled into three countries that use the money for laundering, kickbacks, organized crime activities and cybercrime.

"It's not so much what the crime is; it's who's in charge of it; who's calling the shots. And if it's a single person, he's got to be found out and apprehended. After here in Ireland, we can stress this with Chief Ciccone and see how he responds. Will he see it as something impossible or something that's achievable?"

Ansel had made reservations for a Holiday Inn in Killarney, eleven-miles away. He also rented a car that he drove there and during the ride, Rick entertained three thoughts:

—Refer to what he had placed in his satchel about the four crimes.

—Dismiss the idea that the jerko who had sent the telegrams was the same person who had written the book, *Disaster and More*.

—Read every single poster at airports or hotels or on nearby streets, just as he had done in Balkan territory.

The third thought became a reality at the entrance to the Inn. A poster read:

> Welcome to Killarney. You are in County Kerry, in Southwestern Ireland. We lie in a deep, lake-filled valley in the MacGillicuddy Reeks, our country's largest mountain range, and beside the Lakes of Killarney, which are part of our National Park. Another astounding local feature is the famous Ladies' View, named after Queen Victoria's ladies in waiting.
>
> Our town, also known as Heaven's Reflex, reflects its strong religious and educational history. Killarney was originally established as a church foundation in the 5th or 6th century; and a housing settlement began around 1500. Today, it's a lively hub of activity, with many historical houses, castles, monuments, restaurants, pubs, and more. Here you can explore colorful laneways and fine historic buildings dating back to the days of the landlord or experience the ambience of bustling streets in the town center. Killarney, however, is particularly famous for its history, its cathedral, Ross Castle, Muckross Abbey, and Innisfallen Island with its monastic ruins.
>
> Because of its natural and historical interest, and its close proximity to the Dingle Peninsula and the Ring of Kerry, we are a famous tourist town, Ireland's second most popular after Dublin.

The vote on the Inn itself was a single word: "gorgeous". Their two rooms had expanded balconies overlooking sunny pastures with horses and cows milling around. But they were so exhausted from a full afternoon of interconnecting flight delays, misplaced luggage, and an assortment of trivial but time-consuming incidents, that there was little concentration left to appreciate such views. They just picked at a quiet dinner meal and it was Ansel who spoke up about the upcoming bus tour he had scheduled at Rick's request. It was to begin at eight in the morning.

"That's twelve hours from now," Rick said. There were no objections and they retired for the night. Enthusiastically.

After their morning breakfast, they began a Ring of Kerry bus tour. Right off the bat, Rick could tell it would satisfy his sightseeing need yet not interfere with what they had planned. The weather was cloudy, dark and cool but Gemma their guide offset it with a good sense of humor. An attorney in Ireland, he was an excellent speaker and sat opposite the driver, facing forward, microphone in hand.

He had started by giving a hint of not only what the passengers might expect to see but also of some background history. They would be traveling a 97-mile road that wound among the country's southwest mountainous coast.

"We'll come upon the magnificent MacGilllycuddy Reeks which is a mountain range that contains the highest elevation peak in Ireland. It runs through many passes and valleys along the shore of Dingle Bay."

Rick had read about the range before and had a grammar school friend with the same full name … MacGillycuddy. Because he enjoyed saying the name, he had never used "Mac" as did his classmates.

Gemma continued: "We'll eventually pass through some more landmarks before stopping at the Red Fox Pub for its famous Irish coffee. Then onto the 15th century Bog Village Museum. Next will be Valentia Island which you'll see from the road. The first transatlantic cable was laid between this island and Heart's Content in Newfoundland in 1865. And the first message to an American president by that cable was, "Glory to God in the highest, on earth peace, good will to men".

"Waterville will be next. It's where Charlie Chaplin, his wife and 9 children stayed. She still lives there, and Bob Hope played golf in the vicinity."

He then mentioned an early Christian monastery and a stone fort containing beehive cells. Also, Ladies View, one of the most photographed vistas in Ireland; the crystal Lakes of Killarney; and the wildlife of Killarney National Park.

"Finally, we'll end up where you could take your own pictures. Do include the Lady of Peace Statue." When they returned to the Inn, they had wine in the bar, dinner in the coffee shop and then retired early.

At 9 A.M., they headed through the center of Killarney to a jaunting cart. John was the driver; Rose was the horse; and there were six other passengers. John was a charmer, entertaining them with lots of Irish jokes and tales. They drove through a national park, among an assortment of beautiful trees — some areas dense but some stretches that allowed reflections of the sky onto a narrow lake, making it sparkle.

They stopped at Muckross House where a guide led them throughout, relating unflattering tales about old Queen Elizabeth — terrified of fires so she had to stay on the first floor. Called her a very imperious lady.

They eventually arrived at Cobh but stayed only long enough to read two of the many posters they came across.

> There are few places in Ireland with more poignant memories of the Irish exodus to America than here in Cobh. Hundreds of thousands of poor Irish men and women left this port to sail for America with hopes for a new and better life. For many, the dream came true but for others, the dream ended on board due to terrible conditions suffered on the ships. This is a true harbor town, where the great Transatlantic liners used to

dock up to the 1950s. Do visit the Queenstown Story where you can learn of the emigration from here since the 1800s and the historic role that Cobh played as an important seaport.

This Heritage Center was built in an old Victorian Railway Station and opened in 1933. As you will see, the Queenstown Story is a multimedia exhibition featuring the history of Cobh's origins and tells the story of the great emigration following extreme famine, IRA troubles, and other tragedies. Of 'coffin ships' and 'American wakes'. Of families sending their hardiest children to the U.S., knowing they would never see them again. Of this port being the last one for the Titanic and of the Lusitania being hit off this coast in 1915.

They departed Cobh and after Ansel rented a car, they transferred to the famous village of Blarney, known as the "biggest little village in Ireland". They located the Blarney Stone and Rick ascended to its topside. There, he was assisted in bending backwards to kiss the stone. Then as he straightened up, his eye caught a glimpse of a plaque that read, "You are now endowed with the gifts of eloquence and insight".

"Blarney," he thought, "but who knows for sure?"

Before exiting the Stone, a different sort of triad flashed through his brain like a thunderbolt:

—the plaque message

—any more sightseeing plans

—other mission requests awaiting him at the hospital.

Too much to consider. Or worse — to carry out.

He sat on a side bench, cupped one hand over the other and almost took a smile to a laugh. A decision had been reached within seconds. He would resist scheduling any more sightseeing!

Chapter 17

It was an early Saturday morning when they arrived at Dublin's Herbert Park Hotel, the one Rick had stayed at once before. Out front, they were greeted by a tall man who said his name was Paddy. He was formally dressed in everything green: three-piece suit, shirt, green-striped tie, gloves. Even his shoes. Rick almost asked him to raise his trouser legs a bit so his sock color might be checked.

After confirming that they would be registering there, Paddy helped unload their belongings, said he'd be notifying other employees for assistance and asked that their car be driven into a back parking lot.

"You're just in time for today's two-hour bus tour, if you want to take it," he said.

"Yes, do include us," Rick said after receiving nods from his triad.

But before Ansel drove toward the lot, all four pointed toward a notice on a large white column attached to the front of the hotel. They walked over to read it:

> DUBLIN — the capital of Ireland. It is both elegant and quaint. The city is spread over the valley of the River Liffey and fringed by the Dublin Bay and the Wicklow Mountains. It is itself a colorful and cosmopolitan city. Easily accessed and enjoyed by pedestrian explorers, Dublin's points of interest are many. Pubs, churches, public parks, and museums all make up the city's tapestry. Dublin boasts lovely examples of 18th century architecture, including Georgian mansions, wide streets, and spacious squares. The National Gallery and the National Museum contain artistic treasures and historical artifacts.

> One of the city's most famous landmarks is Trinity College. Founded in 1591, the college has cobbled quadrangles and grey buildings. Its library is home to the Book of Kells, which dates back to the 8th century and is one of the world's oldest manuscripts.
>
> In addition, Dublin is a city that entertains. With theaters, sport facilities, and concert halls, Dublin is a center of Irish and international culture. A lively pub culture also awaits visitors. Dublin's pubs attract artists, students, actors, and writers (building on the city's rich literary tradition). With lively music and a friendly atmosphere, visitor and locals alike come together over pints of Ireland's finest.

The bus tour ran like clockwork. As was the case during the Ring of Kerry tour, a guide spoke throughout it, not only pointing out highlights but spending even more time on historical facts. Some dealt with background, others as though he was teaching a class on international whatever. He did so from the front of the bus, holding a compendium of sorts that his eyes seemed fastened to.

> Ladies and gentlemen. Good morning and thank you for joining us on this panoramic tour. As you can see, we are packed. Now, except in the case of an emergency, we'll be stopping only once. But there's a rest room at the rear of the bus that can accommodate both males and females. Our driver will be driving slowly and will come to a brief stop at each of 10 destinations. Any picture-taking will have to be done through a window, but please be careful because sometimes this bus gets bouncy when changing speeds. I'll announce the name of each destination and then talk some about it. Where we'll get off is near the end of the tour. Trinity College. So let us begin:

—**Luas Tram**. A 2-line light rail/tram which opened just two-years ago and links our center with southern suburbs. An estimated 80,000 people use the tram daily. It's the only mass transit in the country to be operated without government assistance, and among the few in Europe to do so.

—**Grand Canal in Dublin**. It was built in the 18th century to connect our country to the Shannon River and the Irish midlands. It's a major example of the engineering skills of the period. Notice that the towpath on either side of the canal has a rustic character, with terraces of small brick houses, wild foul and swans on the water, and a series of curved 18th-century bridges.

—**Leinster House**. The national parliament of the Republic of Ireland consists of the President of our country and two houses: the Chamber of Deputies and the Senate. All three are based here in Dublin. Both houses meet in the Leinster House which has been the home of Irish parliament since the creation of the Irish Free State in 1922.

Dublin Castle — It's a major Irish governmental complex, formally the fortified seat of British rule here until 1922.

Dublin City Hall — Here, the Council governs Dublin and is presided over by the Lord Mayor of Dublin who is elected for a yearly term and lives in the Mansion House.

St. Patrick's Cathedral — Worship has continued there for 900 years and it is now the National Cathedral for the whole of Ireland. On his journey through Ireland, St. Patrick is said to have passed through here. And in a well close to what you now see, he is reputed to have baptized converts from paganism to Christianity.

James Joyce Center — The Center is dedicated to promoting an understanding of the life and works of James Joyce. Its home is a restored 18th century Georgian townhouse here in Dublin, the city of Joyce's birth and the setting for all his works.

The Center aims—through a program of exhibition, education, outreach and activities—to foster an appreciation of this most remarkable and significant literary figure of the 20th century.

Spire of Dublin — This is the banking, finance and commerce center of Dublin. We have now developed into a world-class center for a wide range of internationally traded financial services.

Temple Bar — This was established in 1840. Live Irish music is played daily and holds Ireland's largest whiskey collection. Last year it won the "Traditional Irish Music Pub of the Year Award.

Trinity College — Our Dublin is the primary center of education with three universities and several other higher education institutions. There are 20 third-level institutes in the city. The University of Dublin is the oldest university here, dating from the 16th century. Its sole constituent college, Trinity College, was established by Royal Charter and was closed to Roman Catholics until the Catholic Emancipation. The Catholic hierarchy then banned Roman Catholics from attending it until 1970. Can you believe that?

The bus stopped and all passengers got off to visit Trinity College. They visited the college's prize possession, the **Book of Kells** display, a world-famous manuscript produced by Celtic Monks in 800 A.D. Next was a brief visit to the second floor which contained **The Long Room**. It was completed in 1732 and housed 200,000 of the Trinity College Library's oldest books and manuscripts, stacked 2 stories high.

Upon exiting the library, Rick heard someone claiming that Napoleon Bonaparte was either murdered or died from inhaling arsenic from wallpaper dye at St. Helena's Longwood. He had slept there for the last 6 years of his life.

“So it was either a murder or an accident,” the person had said, using his last cigarette to light another.

The comments were enough to catch Rick’s attention because the emperor’s fate was the last thing presented to him at the hospital.

Rick then informed Leon of what he had heard.

”It’s not that simple, Rick. In fact, it’s complicated, and I can supply you with the facts. I’ve kept them to myself for too many years.”

“And I’ll add another complication,” Rick said, “but ‘coincidence’ is a better word.”

“Oh?”

“A question from the hospital is: ‘Was Napoleon murdered or not?’”

“And you’ll take the question on?”

“Looking forward to it. It will be the first I **do** take on.”

“Well, as I said, I can help you out on this.”

They both agreed to discuss the issue once they got back to the States.

As they left the bus, the guide’s last remark was, … “not meant to scare you but there’s always gangs from Spain sneaking around. They’re professional pick-pockets so be careful of your purses and belongings.”

“Christ, that’s all we need,“ Rick whispered.

The tour completed, the four agreed that it was worth the time and effort. Rick, especially, felt that there had been no attempt to force any sightseeing and looked forward to calling on Chief O’Brien later in the day. In effect, his thoughts lingered among what they had just seen.

But that was another one at a deeper more complex level: the reaction of the Chief upon hearing of increased money laundering, kickbacks, cybercrime and other organized crime activity. Rick hoped that the reaction was one of appreciation to four men who had ventured to Ireland for an in-person interview in place of a phone call.

Chapter 18

But all that changed dramatically when Rick arrived back at the hotel. No sooner had he settled in than he felt his phone vibrating at his hip. It was Angela calling. Her voice was loud and shrill.

"You've finished with Ireland?" she asked.

"Just about. What's the matter?"

"So it's Rome and Athens next?"

"Yes."

"Absolutely necessary?"

"No. C'mon, Ange. Why the call?"

"There was just a knock on our front door and a paper was slipping under it. It had a message: 'You too, Mrs. Chandler. But who wants a simple shooting?'. I got so scared, I couldn't open the door, or even look out the window. Can you come home?"

Rick's reaction was made much more swiftly than last time. "Oh, no!" he said. "Look, I'll drop everything here and will leave for there immediately. Meanwhile, you stay home from work; lock doors and windows; make sure your Stealth .45 is in your purse and have the purse slung over your shoulder at all times."

"And David Brooks?"

"Yeah, by all means. Call him to stay with you until I get there. Remember, his number is in the nightstand on my side."

"And should I call the police."

"No, have David do the calling."

Rick was holding his phone in one hand and already putting together some outer garments with the other.

"Bye, Ange," he said. "Hang tight. Do what I said and I should be home in five or six hours."

He phoned the others and asked that they meet in his room. There, he detailed Angela's plight and they agreed to leave Ireland as a unit. As usual, Ansel would handle all travel arrangements. "Let's just hope we're lucky with flight time", he said.

Chapter 19

They were. A plane headed for the States took off only 20 minutes after their arrival at the airport.

During the flight, Rick was again seized by many thoughts including another version of the conversation with the Chief:

—Chief: About the crime activity you listed? So what else is new?

—Rick: That's not the point. I've come to warn you of a possible increase in all of it.

—Chief: But why travel all the way to here? Why not use the phone?

—Rick: Not only to here, but also to Rome and Athens. And the reason is that 'in person' has more clout, more body language if you will.

And one other thought: He would resolve something he'd been putting off: fingerprinting. A time for criminalist Walter Sparks.

Once home at mid-morning, and after thanking David, Rick said to a still alarmed Angela:

"So here's how things should shape up now. I'll pick my missions on a more selective basis, traveling here and there for challenges that pique my interest and leaving all others to the four administrative assistants at the hospital. For your foreseeable future, return to work, but before that, review the notes you made after practicing those many times at the firing range.

"Whatever it takes," she replied. "which means whatever you say."

He hesitated before offering a retort: "You know, my love, you're kindest when you've been scared."

She gave him a searching look."Isn't everyone?" she asked.

"No. And I should have been clearer: 'when you've recovered from being scared'. And I think you have, so now I'm calling Leon over to give me some background on Napoleon. I've been thinking about what he said."

"Like what?"

"Well apparently he has some inside information about him."

"You want me present or should I make myself scarce?"

"Definitely present. In fact, take notes. They might help in my handling the subject for the hospital."

Angela suddenly looked as though she was part of some grand design. "So you're phoning him now?" she asked.

"No. One other thing first. I've been putting this off long enough. Both of us should go over to see Sparky about possible fingerprints on those warning sheets. Shouldn't take long."

He put in a call to Sparky and asked if he could see the two of them about examining the sheets for fingerprints. He explained they could arrive at his office within minutes. He answered positively.

Within walking distance of the hospital was the criminalist's office in the Police Department Building. With the two warning sheets in hand, Rick exchanged greetings with friends at the dispatch window and indicated they'd like to confer with Sparky. One announced Rick's arrival as a subdued public address message and he was buzzed into a maze of hallways and interconnecting rooms, each filled with busy employees but most of them taking time off to either wave or smile at Rick.

As they ambled through, steam radiators banged out their familiar but not offensive odor and the floor creaked beneath half partitions. They proceeded directly to the crime lab, past benches of microscopes, chemical bottles, latent fingerprint equipment, piles of wire baskets, swirls of glass tubing, and the brothy smell of petri dishes. They entered the criminalist's corner office without knocking.

Sparky, wearing plastic gloves, sat at a large desk inspecting a handgun through a hand-held microscope.

Rick and Angela converged to shake his hand as if it were for the first time.

"So here are the sheets of paper," Rick said, handing them over.

Sparky led them out to the fingerprint section where they gave their hands a good scrubbing. Then he inked their thumbs over a special pad after saying his own prints wouldn't show because of his gloves. "Just give me a minute or two for the Ninhydrin procedure, and I'll have your answer," he said, retiring to a distant and more lighted area.

Rick always thought the criminalist was a forty-odd throwback to a Western Union clerk in a 1940s B movie: slicked down black hair parted in the middle, wire-framed glasses, gartered shirtsleeves, faded white suspenders.

Sparky returned, shaking his head and saying: "Sorry folks, only **yours** are on the papers."

Just outside the office, Rick said, "So that was that. A complete 'in your face' result, but at least it's done with. To tell the truth, Ange, I'm not sure that learning of someone else's prints on the papers would have served us well anyway."

Chapter 20

Leon arrived at the Chandler home at 10 A.M. Rick couldn't tell if the dark clouds overhead represented what Leon would be saying, or if the favorable weather forecast for the afternoon would be more representative.

"Just buckle down", he told himself.

The men sat at the kitchen table and soon Angela joined them, pencil and notepad in hand. She offered them coffee but they refused.

Leon didn't waste any time. He spread out a raft of notes on the table and said: "It won't take me long to condense what I know about Napoleon. It involves his descendants. And please consider what I say as fact even though I may not have all the answers. You've known me long enough, Rick, to realize I wouldn't mislead you. There'll be many blanks to fill in but, if you will, just accept my overall statements and allow for an assortment of people, places and things."

"We'll accept, my friend, and we appreciate you're taking time to join us here about this."

"Thank you for agreeing to listen. I'll start with citing the importance of DNA in all of this. There are two forms of it; nuclear and mitochondrial. They're both used to identify people, but mitochondrial doesn't degrade as easily, so it's better for those who died hundreds of years ago. The only problem is that it's passed on from generation to generation only in the female line of the family. Well, it was extracted from Napoleon's years-old body some years ago and was also obtained from several other people, which I'll get to in a minute. Then there was an aristocratic French statesman named Talleyrand who hated Napoleon and was thought in some quarters that he murdered him. So he wanted the public to think that the death was due to natural causes.

“Now I’ll toss in a gal named Sophie Bauer who’s been proven to be a direct descendant of the emperor. Sophie lives in Brussels and I’ve twice met with her to straighten things out. What I learned was that she’s indeed a descendant of Napoleon and that she happens to be my half-sister.”

“Your what ?” Rick stammered, leaning back and nearly toppling from his chair. “And that therefore you’re related to Napoleon?” He put his head in his hands and groaned. Then he looked over at Angela through a gap in his fingers. She was nearly gagging but continued to make notes.

“Yes, we are — were — are,” Leon said. “Tracing a lineage like the one I’m talking about involves the feminine side. but it so happens that what’s called ‘the last reference sample’ can be a male. And that’s me.”

Rick, afraid of stumbling on his words, paused before commenting: “Jeez, I had no idea of what to expect and, more than that, of what to learn.”

Leon straightened out his notes but slid one paper aside and half-read from it: “To close this down — and I feel relieved — it took three weeks but way back, an abundant amount of mitochondrial DNA was obtained from Napoleon’s skull. And a reference sample from Sophie Bauer showed a definite match. Furthermore, anthropologists from the French Academy of Sciences confirmed that the openings in the temporal portion of the emperor’s skull were the result of bullet penetration. They couldn’t be sure about a wound on the right being an entry wound or one on the left being an exit wound. If so, however, they believe it to be a case of suicide.”

It had been the first challenge that Rick had selected and the result exceeded his expectations. Not murder, not natural, but possibly suicide.

It was an outcome that he was anxious to relay to the hospital’s Question Division. He did so after being effusive in prolonged thanks to Leon who left for his apartment. Rick’s gaze trailed him while believing that what had just transpired between them had strengthened their already tight relationship.

Then Rick approached Angela and said: “You know how I feel right now? It’s the same as when we went skiing up in Maine on a rainy day that upset us at first, but then, even as the rain became torrential, we yelled out to each other how lucky we were to be there and to continue doing what we were doing. Remember? The rain couldn’t blot out the rolling hills and the uneven ground that surrounded us. Right after that, in the little red barn called ‘Home’, we slugged down some hot chocolate with the many who had earlier called it quits. They quit but we celebrated. Do we have any chocolate to heat up, Ange?”

The hospital’s four-person Question Division congratulated Rick on his work regarding Napoleon and one of them, Zachary, expressed surprise in learning about Leon’s DNA relationship to him.

“What’s next?” he asked, handing Rick a list to look over.

Rick browsed through it and, within a few minutes, gave his decision: “Was there an Eva Perón/Nazi Germany coalition out to loot money and diamonds and hide it all in Swiss banks?”

“You may not appreciate this,” Rick said, “but from now on, I’m picking my destinations carefully. Nowhere too far, nowhere too muddled, nowhere I’d judge as being too dangerous. I’d be traveling to Buenos Aries, Germany and Switzerland. Not too bad I’d say, and as an associated issue, I think it important for people to notice my presence at the destinations. Translation? To be there in person.”

“But there may be other places that might come up,” Zachary said.

“So be it, but for starters, this seems to fit the bill.”

PART THREE

Chapter 21

Even when he was taking cases that were not related to his current undertakings, his initial problem was where to begin. Maybe it should be backwards in this case — that is, starting with Switzerland, then follow with Germany and Buenos Aires. Were looted monies and diamonds being hidden in Swiss banks? Were they being blackmailed or intimidated or something like that?

Rick didn't know why but he suddenly thought of the delegation of armed Swiss guards protecting the Vatican area. His mouth edged into a grin as he decided on what had to be done. Initially visit Zurich, Switzerland's capital and where most of its banks had their headquarters. And then, give the Vatican some further thought, realizing that 50 % of the Swiss population is Catholic. Necessary to go there, too?

He gathered up his triad and they headed for Zurich, uncertain of whom to see there until he had asked Leon.

"It's a man named Albany. John Albany. I've dealt with him before and I'm sorry I have to do so again. But he's the Swiss Banking Czar, main man within the banking industry there."

"And I take it you and he didn't get along," Rick said.

"That's putting it mildly. He's just a testy person. You'll see," Leon said back.

"Well, we'll deal with it," Rick countered. "Bad among bads."

"What's **that**?"

"I'd guess we all have had to deal with a share of the bad people in the world."

"Yes. Well put. But there's one thing I liked about Zurich: the so-called Sunrise Tower in center city. That's where his office is. And speaking of his office, his secretary is more friendly. She was at least decent. Name's Mildred. I'll phone ahead and ask if she'll squeeze us in."

During the flight to the Zurich Airport, Rick removed a folder from his satchel and, for the umpteenth time, read some extractions he'd collected about Evita and her husband; about Nazi history; and about Swiss banking:

> First of all, some reports date back to the days of Eva Perón. That she offered asylum to some heinous Nazis. Secondly, that some Nazis hid there in Argentina, changing their names and faking a normal life. With her help. But others remained criminals in many ways, or they escaped to Belarus if they found that some Argentinians were growing suspicious of them. And third, that many valuable books, diamonds and other jewels were plundered by the Nazis from that country. Its capital is Minsk and it's a city that differs so much from the rest of the country. That's why it should be visited, sooner or later.

> In June of 1947, Argentina's first lady Eva Perón left for a glittering tour of Europe. The glamourous ex-actress was feted in Spain, kissed the ring of Pope Pious XII at the Vatican, and hobnobbed with the rich-and-famous in the mountains of Switzerland.
>
> Known as "Evita" by her adoring followers, she was superficially on a trip to strengthen diplomatic, business and

cultural ties between Argentina and important leaders of Europe. But there was a parallel mission behind the high-profile trip, one that has contributed to a half century of violent extremism in Latin America.

According to records now emerging from Swiss archives and the investigations of Nazi hunters, an unpublicized side of Evita's world was coordinating the network for helping Nazis relocate in Argentina. This new evidence of Evita's cozy ties with prominent Nazis corroborates the long-held suspicion that she and her husband, Gen. Juan Perón, laid the groundwork for a bloody resurgence of Fascism across Latin America in the 1970s and 80s.

Besides blemishing the Evita legend, the evidence threatens to inflict more damage on Switzerland's image for plucky neutrality. The international banking center is still staggering from disclosures about wartime collaboration with Adolph Hitler and Swiss profiteering off his Jewish victims. The archival records indicate that Switzerland's assistance to Hitler's henchmen didn't stop with the collapse of the Third Reich.

During World War II, General Perón, a populist military leader, made no secret of his sympathies for Mussolini's Italy and Hitler's Germany.

Even as the Third Reich crumbled in the spring of 1945, Perón remained a pro-fascist stalwart, making available more than 1,000 blank passports for Nazi collaborators fleeing Europe.

With Europe in chaos and the Allies near victory, tens of thousands of ranking Nazis dropped out of sight, tried to mix in with common refugees and began plotting escapes from Europe to Argentina across clandestine "ratlines".

By 1946, the first wave of defeated fascists was settling into new Argentine homes. The country also was rife with rumors that the thankful Nazis had begun to repay Perón by bankrolling his campaign for the presidency, which he won with his stunning wife at his side.

In 1947, Perón was living in Argentina's presidential palace and was hearing pleas from thousands of other Nazis desperate to flee Europe. The stage was set for one of the most troubling boatlifts in human history.

The archival records reveal that Eva Perón stepped forward to serve as Gen. Perón's personal emissary to this Nazi underground. Already, Evita was an Argentine legend.

Born in 1919 as an illegitimate child, she became a prostitute to survive and to get acting roles. As she climbed the social ladder, lover by lover, she built up deep resentments toward the traditional elites.

As a mistress to other army officers, Evita fashioned herself as the "queen of the poor", the protector of those she called "mis descamisados" … "my shirtless ones". She created a foundation to help the poor buy items from toys to houses.

But her charity extended, too, to her husband's Nazi allies.

Chapter 22

Based on what he had learned, Rick had little doubt that he would be put off by John Albany. But he would suffer through it anyway, hoping to receive even a stitch of useful information.

Rick had also learned that the Sunrise Tower was one of the few high-rise buildings in central Zurich. He and his triad headed there after landing.

Leon's call to Albany's secretary, Mildred, had worked, for she led the way to the banking czar's office immediately upon their arrival. She warned, however, that because of his busy schedule, their time with him would be limited.

A set of ebony doors opened onto an elongated balcony. The men looked down over a railing and saw a number of interconnected rooms, each occupied with a woman who was working at a computer and never looked up. Each wore a green blouse whose backside bore an emblem of a dollar bill.

Mildred opened a door for them and left. They walked in and couldn't believe what they found there. Or didn't. As plain an office as could be imagined. And as plainly dressed an important man as could be imagined. There was only one desk and one chair; no tables, book shelves, computer, printer, or copier.

The man was seated at the desk and they knew he was the right guy for he wore a cap with the name "Albany" attached above its visor. He appeared about forty.

Never standing to greet them and hardly looking up, he said in a distant voice, “Good day. I have a few minutes for you.”

He seemed tall and thin, was casually dressed in a green shirt and no tie or jacket. Square-rimmed glasses hung from his neck. His eyes were blue but inactive and his facial features appeared crunched into his skull, giving him the look of one unable to smile. And he didn’t. He kept checking his wrist watch.

Rick introduced himself and the others and was about to indicate why they were there when Albany said, “I know why you’re here … Mildred told me … so let’s get on with it, shall we?” It was as if it were a no-nonsense question.

Rick, though standing, stiffened his legs and replied: “Okay. Are Swiss banks dealing in stolen money and if so, does it go all the way back to Eva Perón?”

“What do you mean “dealing’?”

“Receiving; accepting; storing, No matter the source.”

“What business is it of yours? And sorry anyway. Banking matters belong to the depositors and no one else. So check some other way.”

“How’s that?”

“Check with Eva.”

“But she’s dead!”

“Then check with her descendants.”

“Thanks a lot on that score,” Rick said, his legs still stiffened. “So another one: was Pope Francis somehow tied in with Swiss banks. Remember, some of your Army serve as guards at the Vatican.”

“I remember. So go bother the Pope. And speaking of ‘go’, I must ask that you leave. I have more pressing things on my mind.”

On the way to the door, Rick turned and said, "I'd give you the kind of bye-bye you deserve, but I don't swear."

The encounter lasted a mere two minutes. "What came out of that anyway," he asked the triad.

"N'aboutir a rien" Fran said.

"What's that mean?" Rick asked.

"French for, 'to come to nothing'," Fran answered proudly.

Rick elected not to get into word translations and instead said, "Let's take stock, folks. Our goal was to visit Argentina, Germany and Switzerland in that order, but then we decided to start backwards. So next it should be time to visit Germany and then Buenos Aires, but I think now we should eliminate traveling to either country because it seems like it would be duplication. But I **do** say that we haven't talked about the Jewish state. About various groups looking into the question of what happened to money deposited in Swiss banks by non-Swiss Jews who were later murdered in the Holocaust. And speaking of that horrible period, what happened to monies deposited by various Nazi groups in those Swiss banks?"

"May I add my two cents?" Leon asked, raising his hand as if he were a school boy.

"Please do," Rick said. "I've been doing too much thinking aloud."

"I think we've answered what you selected from the hospital's Question Division. A Counsel call."

"And we've done it satisfactorily," Fran added. "So I'd vote to go home."

"And rest a few days," Leon said.

Rick nodded.

Chapter 23

Angela had left for work just before the doorbell rang. Rick, still in his pajamas, zigzagged over to open the door. Two husky men stood there, pointing guns in his direction. They wore face masks and towered over him. "Don't move," one barked.

Before Rick had a chance to unleash one of his karate chops, they wrestled him to the floor and injected a needle into his arm.

He lost consciousness immediately but awoke a few minutes later in a nearby barn. He was tied at the wrists, waist and ankles but his mind felt clear.

In distinct English, the man said, "We could have disposed of you on the spot but we didn't want it that way. We wanted you 'out of it' at first and then have you see what would be happening to you. So we'll carry you there now. It's a river running near Bridgeport and there's a long steep waterfall there. It's where you get dumped. Dumped. Hear that?"

While the man was speaking, Rick was able to loosen his right arm and wrist some … enough to reach into his pants' pocket without notice. And enough to reach his container of Mace. While turning his head to the side, he was able to shoot a hefty spray in their direction. They wiped their eyes and dropped to the floor.

Rick struggled free, grabbed their guns and yanked off their masks. He recognized neither one but believed they were Americans. American bums who'd been hired. Then keeping one gun pointed in their direction, he side-stepped to the nearest phone to call the police.

It was an incident he wasn't surprised had taken place. And he decided that from that point on he would keep the 9 mm. in his ankle rig even during a night's sleep. Even while figuring he never had a chance of using it on the bums.

Internalizing, he concluded: "Guess I'll have to live with this sort of thing and be on the ready. But maybe I can stop once the stupid Dracula thing gets resolved. He's nothing but a fake anyway! And this near-waterfall event? Keeping it to myself for now."

Chapter 24

Once through in Switzerland, the group had returned to the states, disbanded and gone their separate ways. Rick received assurances that they'd be available when needed.

In fact, he went right home, holding off on going to the hospital to give his latest mission report. When he finally did, however, he was greeted warmly. The administrators informed him that there were plenty of requests received and the choice was his. He indicated he would delay the choice for a few days.

Rick had just re-entered his home when one of its phones rang. It was longtime friend, Thatcher Drinkwell, calling. He was the Constable in far-off St. Helena and also happened to be an histarian. One of its leaders, in fact.

After Rick succumbed to some long-winded questions and answers, Drinkwell finally got to the reason for the call: "My fellow histarians have told me about your new job at Hollings Hospital and about the service you perform there regarding answering people's non-medical questions by traveling all over the world. And after much research on your part, you came up with a conclusion that Napoleon Bonaparte committed suicide."

As per his custom, the constable didn't often allow those he was addressing to interject any comments. He went right on to add: "Well, I have something to say about that, but it can't be over the phone. It won't change history but what can? Is it worth a trip here? It's a long way, I know, but it'll pay off. I'm sure of it."

The ensuing pause was the kind that Rick always interpreted as the one where an answer was expected.

"Thatch, I see. And truth be known, you're absolutely right about my traveling a lot. But I'm taking some time off now and although you're miles and miles away, this would be a different kind of travel. If I were to say yes, I can bring along my so-called triad? They're my good friends and confidants."

"Of course. Your answer is 'yes' then?"

"Yes. You're far off, but I always liked the trip. And with my triad along, it won't be boring. Also, I don't think Angela will mind. She's so tied up with her work."

"Excellent! But before you take off, could you read up on a guy named Talleyrand? You've heard of him?"

"Yes and I still have the draft of a white paper about him. I've read the first part but that's all. It's too long."

"No, no. Read the whole thing since it all bears on what I'll be saying when you arrive here. Because of my histarian status, I can't say more than that over the phone, but do read the whole thing, no matter how long it is. Okay?"

"Okay."

"So I'll be seeing you and your friends in a day or two. Have a good trip."

Rick found the white paper that dealt with Talleyrand during the Napoleonic years. He curled up on his recliner and read:

> Talleyrand (1754-1838) was a French statesman who was born into an aristocratic family in Paris. Witty, crafty and complex, he became one of the most controversial, influential

and fascinating figures in French history. But his standing with the emperor was erratic at best.

Talleyrand's full name was Charles Maurice de Talleyrand-Perigord, Prince de Benevent. His clubfoot rendered him unable to enter a military career and marked him by his parents as unfit to carry on the family lineage. Early on they stripped him of his birthright and any anticipated inheritance. Because he could not follow in the traditional military footsteps of the Talleyrand dukes, he embarked on a religious career, a move acceptable to his family and one which, they felt, would bring him some degree of social standing, at least. At age sixteen, he began studies for holy orders at the seminary of St. Sulpice and nine years later received his degree from the Sorbonne and was ordained a priest.

He rose rapidly within ecclesiastical circles, combining both theological and political aspirations. But even during his student days, he exhibited a thinly veiled revolutionary philosophy. This eventually became more overt and after participating in activities considered radical by the Church (celebrating mass on the Champs de Mars to commemorate the anniversary of the storming of the Bastille; spearheading the confiscation of Church property for the national government), he was excommunicated in 1791.

Two year later, he fled to the United States after learning of a warrant for his arrest for unspecified charges. He spent three years in the Massachusetts area working in commodity trading and real estate speculation. The warrant was revoked in 1796 and he returned to France where, with the assistance of friends in high positions, he was appointed Foreign Affairs Minister of the ruling assembly. At about this time, he caught the eye of Napoleon Bonaparte and, each man sensing the political merits of a friendship, they became allies. There followed a series of key political appointments granted by Napoleon between 1804 and 1814 including Grand Chamberlain and Vice-elector of the

Empire; sovereign Prince of Benevento (a small principality taken from the Pope); and representative of France at the Congress of Erfurt.

But Talleyrand was also involved in some shady and sinister developments during this same period and his relationship with the emperor began to deteriorate. They were at odds on several military and foreign policy matters. He publicly condemned what he called the crude treatment of Prussia. He opposed the Franco-Russian Alliance and, later, the attack on Russia. From 1812 on, he became a Russian secret agent. In effect, he became a spy for Russia, Austria and England, accepting bribes from them to reveal Napoleon's secrets. He even demanded bribes from the United States. His firm stand against the Spanish campaign so infuriated Joseph Fouche, the head of Napoleon's secret police, that it helped convince the emperor that he was plotting against him. This provided the spark for Napoleon's famous depiction of Talleyrand as "a piece of dung in a silk stocking".

Because of his perpetually shifting loyalties, especially during the French Revolution (1789-1799) — sometimes supporting the revolution, the empire or the monarchy … historians continue to debate whether the man was a consummate diplomat who valued France's survival at any cost or a mercenary who selfishly sought out opportunities to "feather his own nest". One thing was certain: he was a voluptuary who had a passion for sexual liasons. It is said that he had four illegitimate children including the painter, Eugene Delacroix, and possibly one who was conceived while he lived in the United States. He was furthermore a gourmet and in early 1800 owned the elegant Château Haut-Brion in Bordeaux. In this connection, he hired outstanding culinary personnel and was reputed to acquire only the finest tea and spices directly from the British East India Tea Company.

Chapter 25

The four men began the long and complicated journey to St. Helena the next morning. Ansel had arranged a flight to London and Leon had rented a car to drive them to Brize Norton Airbase, an hour away. Then an R.A.F. plane flew them to Ascension Island, a three hour flight. After a seven-hour wait, a royal mail ship set sail for a 700-mile, day-and-a–half trip to Jamestown.

They communicated little during the ordeal. Rick felt as though he was part of a multinational secret operation during which friends were suspect, light fixtures were bugged and all military captains and sea captains were possible espionage agents. But he got over it.

To occupy his time during the sailing, he decided to read about what awaited them from the book he had written, *The Strange Death of Napoleon Bonaparte*. He had written it many years ago — 15 at least — had forgotten much of it, and labeled it more of a review. He promised himself that he wouldn't be critical of his own writing in any way.

In it, the protagonist was Paul D'Arneau and his friends were Vincent and Sylvie.

He took the book out of his satchel, leafed through its pages until he found a good place to begin, and with minor extractions here and there, he read the following:

> A half hour later, Paul put in a call to Jean. It was around 6 a.m. in the States. As he waited for the connection, he considering distancing himself from the mission for a while, yet hoped that something would come along to change his mind. And

it did, in the form of Jean's persuasive words, a complete reversal of what she had said four days earlier.

"Hello, Jean?"

"Paul! I thought I wouldn't hear from you for days. Where are you?"

"Elba. We're leaving for Paris late this afternoon. I decided to cut short our stay here."

Once again he summarized what had happened on the "gutted road". He even told her about the pistol and ankle rig Vincent had given him. Jean said nothing. Paul felt some facial blotches and wondered why none had appeared during the confrontation there. Were his emotions and their effect on his nervous system playing tricks on him. Ever since early boyhood, he had come to predict with great accuracy when he would turn blotchy.

He made a point of mentioning Napoleon, Lady Beckett and the illegitimate child and then said, "I don't know, Jean. I think I'm all screwed up. This is getting to me: the stalking car, the kidnapping, the note, the mysterious call Vincent got, and now this. For a moment there, I was thinking of bowing out.

"Wait a second. What note? What call?"

"Oh, someone left a warning under my door the other day. Then a couple of days later, some guy called Vincent and told him I should mind my own business. I didn't say anything because I didn't want to alarm you, but since the armed men in their cutesy hoods came into the picture, all bets are off."

"What did the note say?"

"Leave Paris, *tout de suite*."

"Listen to me," Jean said. "What did you do when Vincent gave you his pistol and the holster?"

"I brought it back here to the room and strapped it to my ankle."

"And extra bullets?"

"In my pocket."

"So there you are: dilemma solved."

"What's **that** supposed to mean?"

"Paul darling, you can't turn away now. Intellectually and emotionally you can handle it. All the negative stuff may just be attempts to scare you off, but the fact that you armed yourself tells me you're ready for anything. You just have to be extremely careful from now on. And you have Vincent. God bless him." Her voice quivered. "I know you, Paul. You're not a quitter, so go on to St. Helena as planned. Please!"

He couldn't believe it. He clearly remembered his first call home, when Jean had expressed so many misgivings about the mission. And now, the reversal. A reversal that made her voice more cogent.

"You may be right," he said. "I mean whoever thought I'd be packing a gun. Thanks, Jean. What is they say? I needed that. And I love you."

He ended their conversation with a reminder that she wouldn't hear from him for several days.

"Maybe not until we get back from Helena."

In spite of the encouraging call, Paul was still glad they were leaving Elba. True, there were sites he'd wanted to visit but the chances were slim that anything significant would have been uncovered: the old adage about a needle in the haystack.

He made copious but disorganized notes about the information he'd garnered on Elba. That occupied the first hour of the flight back to Paris, a point when he thought he was too restless to sleep. Four hours later, minutes before touchdown, he found he was wrong.

Leon was waiting at the airstrip, standing on an open platform adjoining a shabby, window-laden building. He wore the biggest trench coat Paul had ever seen. He would have wagered it was custom-made.

"Welcome back, my boy," Leon said, "or should I say boys and girl, our island travelers?"

Paul began sheepishly: "Leon, please forgive …"

"No need to explain. I'm certain that another day on Elba wouldn't have yielded much more anyway. St. Helena is the real place for the nuggets."

After Leon had shaken their hands, Sylvie and Vincent led the way toward the entrance. Leon signaled Paul to hang back. "I realize it's not exactly warm," he said, "but I want to add to what I said on the phone a while ago. In your travels around the world in your, shall we say, your secondary job …"

"Primary now."

"Primary. You must have come across people of all kinds including double-dealers, undercover operatives, sharks, shakedown artists."

"Yeah, all kinds, but none with deadly weapons,"

"None that you could see."

"Paul wiggled his toes, feeling the ankle rig.

"So? Now you see them."

"Believe me, Leon, I respect what you're driving at but it wasn't that I was shook. Maybe surprised. It was that I didn't expect it where it occurred. On a godforsaken imitation of a road near a bunch of ruins. And that's not the whole story. Couple it with Sylvie's kidnapping, with the warning note, with the cars trailing me, all of this in a few short days. But I'm okay now. In fact I'm more determined than ever. As long as I know the ground rules, or lack thereof, and I now know them, I say, 'Bring on the bastards'."

Paul spoke as if he had a message for the whole world to hear. "While we're on the subject," he said, "one other thing: I'd swear those guys were Mafia."

"They no doubt were. Hired guns."

"Well I've never dealt with them directly before, but that's okay too. I'll be on my toes."

Leon peered through one of the windows. "Sylvie and Vincent look impatient," he said, "but one other thing before we join them. You must have your own network, don't you? I ask because if you do, it may be time to rely on them. For tips, don't you know."

Paul felt the cold through his thin jacket but wanted to hear more, away from the others. "Tips?" he asked. "How do you mean? For leads?"

"That and warnings of people lurking. Your antennas. Here in France, in England, in Italy, wherever you go. I guess I'm asking if you have some contacts of your own."

"Some."

"I suppose you could call it a network?"

"I suppose."

"Global?"

"Possibly."

"Sizeable?"

"Possibly."

"I'll take that as a yes on all counts. So you've verified what we at Vérité have discovered."

Paul scratched his finger. It felt so good that, considering the circumstances, he scratched it again. "Sounds like I've been vetted," he said.

"You've been thoroughly vetted. That's not a bad thing, is it? As I've assured you in the past, you have exactly what it takes to accomplish what we've engaged you to do."

"Paul didn't answer. He smiled wryly, opened the door and allowed Leon to walk in first.

The truth was that Paul had very little of what he would term a network: a few contacts here and there, a few gratified clients, a few fellow hunters of missing treasures.

Inside, Leon stopped to ask, "Can you trust them?"

"Some of them. You mean regarding what the mission's about?"

"Precisely."

"No need to. I could just say I'm working on something important and potentially dangerous and let it go at that, If I have to explain at all."

"As you wish. I'm simply trying to make it easier for you."

"I know that and I appreciate it. Believe me, I'm ready for anything." Paul held back a qualifying phrase, however: "At least I hope so."

"Fine. And you're ready for St. Helena?"

"Ready. Okay to leave tomorrow or do we wait till Wednesday?"

"I've already checked and it's no problem arriving a day earlier than we'd planned. I've made arrangements with both the R.A.F. and the folks at the Farm Lodge Hotel. It's fifteen minutes from the center of Jamestown. Very nice, very private, I'm told. As for Thatcher Drinkwell, he'll probably be at the Police Service Building.

Paul took out his pad and scribbled in the names of both buildings.

He didn't take Leon's advice lightly. Upon arrival in his hotel room, however, he decided to take it one step further. He recalled having traveled to the Netherlands three or four years ago to help locate two misplaced paintings, a Rembrandt and a Pieter de Hooch. They were found but Paul had played a minor role. He had worked closely, however with one Victor Frelinghuyens, an art dealer in Amsterdam who had once casually mentioned that organized crime was prevalent in his city because members of the Yugoslav Mafia had moved in. He had even met with some of them. Since then, Paul had often speculated about possible ties between the dealer and those members. There was a favor to be returned because he had waved his fee in exchange for a promise to assist in any of Paul's future work in Europe.

"Hello, Victor?"

"Yes, this is Victor."

"Paul D'Arneau here."

"Paul! My goodness. How are you?" They exchanged stories about their past joint venture, laughing along the way. Paul made a point of mentioning his dismissal from Yale and the welcome beginning of a full-time career in treasure hunting.

"I don't know exactly how to put this, Victor, but I'll take a stab at it. And forgive me if I sound too presumptuous."

"Come now, Paul, Anything at all; you know that."

"Okay. I'm about to travel to St. Helena on a job I accepted that might carry with it some … ah … dangers."

"St. Helena, the island? Napoleon and all that?"

"Yes." Paul paused to find the right words. "Now, would you be in a position to arrange for some underworld figures to look out for my welfare and that of my two traveling companions? That is, if any exist there? I don't want to hire private body guards. This is very hush-hush and the privates don't have the same code as, say, the Mob. Plus different factions of the Mob recognize each other and that would help in tipping me off about some … I hate to say it … some strike aimed at one of us. Or of keeping the bad guys at bay."

Silence at the other end prompted Paul to shift the one-way conversation somewhat. "I can't believe I'm talking this way, Victor, and I do hope I'm being clear."

Finally a response: "You're being very clear. This is not the first time I've been asked to help in the exact same way. And yes, I **do** have a contact on Helena. I've vacationed there several times. He has some friends who are just the type you have in mind. Give me the particulars of when you'll arrive, where you'll be staying, when you expect to leave, and of course the names of your companions. Then leave the rest to me. The man's name is Smit-Jules Smit. One way or another he will contact you. There will be a red convertible waiting dockside. I'll see to it that the driver wears a white cap. He'll take you and your friends wherever you want to go during your stay there."

Paul gave him the information, thanked him profusely and indicated he would be notified about how things went, "if I make it out alive."

"Don't worry," Victor said, "my man is most dependable. If he works it the same as before, he'll have three of his pals helping him. Most of the Saints, as the islanders refer to themselves, are dark-skinned. Some darker than others. These three tend to stand out. They're all fair and blond … two men and a woman. They'll be, as we say, 'In and out; around and about'. If there are individuals after your skin … ah … forgive me. I mean who are interested in you. Having these people there will fend them off. The underworld on St. Helena isn't large so they all know one another. They realize that if they dare hurt you, there will be retribution. Plus you've heard it before and it does exist: there's a certain honor among thieves."

Paul disregarded the honor reference. "What you mean is that if I get killed, someone will get even? Quite a comfort." He managed a laugh.

"That's not the point. It's a deterrent thing."

Paul was mildly reassured but also had some more than mild doubts about the whole deal.

> *This is one for the books: a fired college professor with a gun strapped to his ankle, in the middle of nowhere, about to be protected from the underworld, while he investigates the strange death of one of history's greatest generals. Surreal!*
>
> He wasn't certain why he believed the deal would work effectively only if no one else knew about it. Not Sylvie, not Leon, not even Vincent. A question perhaps of too many people "in" on a secret and therefore too many chances for a slip-up? But aside from the effectiveness and slip-ups, he didn't want others to think he was in bed with criminal elements. After all, he had to consider assignments that might come his way in the future: life without Napoleon.

Paul was preparing for bed when something suddenly dawned on him. He perched on the edge of the bed and phoned Leon.

"I forgot to ask how we get back from Helena," he said.

"Oh that?" Leon replied. "Yes, certainly, totally slipped my mind. Sorry. It's been taken care of. I've chartered a special ship to leave from Capetown and arrive at St. Helena four days later, five at most. The the whole trip in reverse; Ascension, R.A.F. and so on. The only hitch is, if you want to leave the island sooner than two or three days after arrival, you won't be able to. Does this sound reasonable to you?"

"No, not really," Paul said, disturbed. "If possible though, I'd like for an emergency plan to be in place. We know what happened on Elba. What if we **need** to leave earlier than anticipated?"

Paul waited a quiet few seconds and then tapped on the receiving end of the phone. A moment later, Leon said, "Well I hope that's not the case but, okay, to be ready for that decision, let's do it this way. I'll contact Thatcher Drinkwell and he'll have a separate ship on alert to depart at any time you want. It's asking a lot of him but I'm confident he's up to it Is that better?"

"Much better. I have this funny feeling but I'm sure Elba sensitized me."

The three island travelers began their long trip to St. Helena. They were provided with separate cabins that were unexpectedly roomy and contained a lower and fold-away upper berth, large window, two wardrobe units, an armchair, a dressing table with an over-lighted mirror and a bathroom with shower. They were informed that meals would be available.

The lone exception to their relative silence was an encounter between Paul and Sylvie aboard ship. Once again she made a move that left little doubt about her intentions. It began when Paul answered a knock on his cabin door several hours after dinner. Sylvie stood there, smiling roguishly. And once again, she wore a robe, this time black. And she carried a leather bag. *But why the high heels?* She entered and checked that the door was shut behind her.

"Thought you might like some company," she said. Her breath smelled of alcohol.

"You've had a drink?" he asked with a tinge of jealously. "Where'd you get the stuff and what is it?"

"I brought it along. I was sure we'd never have anything as nice on a damn mail boat."

"So what is it that's so nice?"

"Armagnac Napoleon."

"What's that?"

"A cognac but not as dry. Want some?"

Paul didn't hesitate. "Yes, by all means. I like the Napoleon part."

Sylvie reached into the bag and withdrew a small colorful bottle and a wine glass. She filled the glass with the cognac and handed it to Paul but not before taking a small sip from it and running her tongue around her lower lip.

"C'mon over," he said. "Have a seat. Aren't you having a drink of your own?"

"I had enough in my room." She stepped closer to him while he took in the drink's bouquet and swished the cognac around. As he did so, he never took his eyes off her.

"Careful, don't bump into me," he said. He downed the drink in one swallow.

She moved even closer and breathed, "But I want to get close enough to see if you take tiny gulps, or big gulps". She corrected herself, raising her voice. "That's dumb. If they're tiny, they're not gulps. My mistake."

"Your mistakes are charming," Paul said. He sidestepped her and signaled for a refill. "What the hell," he added. "I'm tired of being cautious all the time."

She complied.

The last Paul remembered was the glass being refilled several more times and leading her to his bed and pulling her onto him.

The following morning after separate breakfasts, Paul confronted her. "Ah, tell me," he whispered. "What happened last night?"

"Nothing," she said, peering down her nose.

"Literally?"

"You fell asleep. Life is whizzing by, you know."

Paul thought of Jean back home but had to admit he was in a quandary over Sylvie's obvious desire. "It may come to pass, Syl, but please, not on this trip."

"No one's ever called me Syl."

"Now someone has."

He picked up a flyer he had obtained outside the ship's galley. Titled *St. Helena and Napoleon*, it was one in a pile available to all passengers. Other piles dealt with services on the island such as banking, transport, communications, immigration, shopping, and medical care. He browsed through the flyer and realized he knew nearly everything in it, having written so extensively about the emperor. Nonetheless, he returned to the beginning and reviewed it word for word:

> St. Helena, a British island in the South Atlantic, is situated 1,200 miles off the southwest coast of Africa and 700 miles southeast of Ascension Island. The Portuguese discovered St. Helena in 1502 but it became part of Great Britain in 1673. The island is approximately ten miles by seven miles in size or about half the size of Napoleon's former home in Exile, Elba. Rough and mountainous, it is composed mainly of volcanic wasteland. The highest peaks, Diana's Peak and Mount Actaeon, rise more than 1,000 feet above sea level. An area of past volcanic activity is Sandy Bay which contains fertile soil, ideal for the island's fruit and vegetable production. Three columns of Basalt in this area are called Lot, Lot's Wife and Asses Ears.
>
> The island's only port and village is Jamestown, its capital. Its population is about 5,000, principally Europeans, Africans and East Indians. Its main bay is called James Bay.

Rick thought by now that he'd be tired of reading his own words. Granted they were many years old, yet they were still his. But by doing so, he'd developed a strange feeling of having disengaged himself from the present and transporting himself to a distant time. The time of its writing. It was both "then" and "now" and he continued to find the words interesting.

The chief crops are flax and potatoes. For a century or more, the flax was used to make mail bags for British post offices but this process has declined because of the availability of cheaper synthetic materials. Other industries there include fish curing and the manufacture of lace and fiber mats.

For many years, it was an important port of call for Portuguese sailors to replenish their supplies and to receive medical attention. At one time, both the British and Dutch claimed the island as their own as they visited it on their voyages to India. In 1659, the East India Company colonized the island. Fourteen years later, the Dutch attacked and took over the island but the British retook it within six months.

Napoleon Bonaparte of course was its most famous resident. After his defeat at Waterloo, he signed a second abdication at the Èlysée Palace. Three weeks later, he surrendered himself to the captain of *H.M.S. Bellerophon* which took him to Plymouth. From there, he embarked on the *H.M.S. Northumberland* bound for St. Helena, arriving October 15, 1815. He was allowed a retinue of thirty people. Napoleon stayed at a small house, the Briars, while his eventual home, Longwood House, was being readied. Shortly thereafter, he moved into Longwood and lived there until his death.

Three frigates and eight other vessels continually patrolled James Bay or were kept on standby. Gun emplacements and guard posts were established throughout the island.

A year later, Sir Hudson Lowe was appointed governor of St. Helena and it quickly became apparent that he and Napoleon had little respect for one another.

Napoleon died there on May 5, 1821. The cause and manner of death remain in dispute. Some claim he was poisoned by arsenic, either intentionally or by accident. Others state he died of stomach cancer as his father did. He was buried in the island's Sane Valley where his body remained until 1840. It was then transported to Paris and currently lies in the Hotel des Invalides.

It was a sketchy article but Paul filled in the gaps. The 1815 to 1821 St. Helena period was his least favorite in the saga of Napoleon Bonaparte but now, soon to set foot on the island for the first time, he reflected on what he might discover. More specifically, if Elba were any kind of reference point, what on earth would Helena bring?

Paul was on deck when the ship headed into its southerly approach to James Bay. He had seen numerous photographs of the island but when it came into view in the slightly hazy light, he was amazed at how photography had failed to capture its sheer darkness. From a distance, it resembled a massive black iceberg. As they sailed closer, he could make out its irregular upper border and what he considered a "slit"down the middle where a collection of white buildings stood. There were more off to the right on higher ground.

Upon docking at 8:20 a.m., Vincent called Paul aside and said, "I've never asked you directly, but what's your agenda here?"

Paul scratched at his temple. "What else? Surprise: another interview! That and a visit to Longwood; maybe to Napoleon's grave site; and to wherever else Drinkwell recommends."

"But couldn't we have simply phoned the guy and saved all this time and effort?"

"Believe me, Vincent, that would have been my choice but you know histarians. They release information only if the conversation is eyeball to eyeball. So we had no choice."

They caught up to Sylvie who was the first to disembark.

"Okay, you two," Paul said. "Let's stick close together while we're here."

"Which is how long?" Sylvie asked.

"As long as it takes," Paul replied. He chose not to mention the "emergency ship".

"That's what I was afraid of," she said.

"Come now. I thought you were looking forward to this trip."

"I was until last night."

"What happened last night?" Vincent asked.

"I had a bad dream."

"And I guess I didn't mention it," Paul added, glad that Vincent was nearby, "but Leon arranged transportation for us. Either of you see a red car?"

"There's one," Vincent said, pointing toward a parking space a few shops up. A street sign indicated, "Napoleon Street", difficult to read in the eye-blinding light of the morning. It appeared to be the main and only street in town. Quiet, narrow and congested with all makes of cars, their colors in sharp contrast to the light buildings hugging the street. Most of the buildings were one-storied with cement facades. Sidewalks were similarly congested with dawdling people, none of whom looked suspicious. Paul had made it a point to check.

A tall man emerged from a red convertible and walked up to them. He wore sunglasses and a white cap. "Is one of you Dr. Paul D'Arneau?" he asked with a slight accent. Paul couldn't pinpoint the country, probably European.

"I am," Paul said.

"May I speak with you privately?"

"Certainly." Paul followed the man for a short distance, just outside of earshot.

The man extended a hand and Paul shook it. "Good morning," the man said, taking off his cap. His hair was strikingly blond, his face mottled and his bare, muscular arms tanned. "I am a professional driver. I am Jules Smit."

"You?" Paul exclaimed. He glanced at Sylvie and Vincent who seemed to be having their own conversation. Lowering his voice he said, "But I thought this would be secret."

"It will be just that. Do not worry. I will drive you around at your disposal. And my people have been alerted. They will not be conspicuous."

"Will I be able to identify them in the background?"

"Maybe. Maybe not. But their skin is light. Especially the men's Two: Gregor and Gunnar. There is also a young lady: Katrien. Sweetheart of Gunnar. Very attractive, but do not let that fool you. I would not like to fight with her. You lose your eyes."

Another handshake followed, this time Paul initiating it.

When he moved away from Jules and rejoined the others, Vincent said, "What was *that* all about?"

"He wanted to know where we'll be staying and for how long. Said he'd be at our disposal at all times."

Rick still did not recall most of what he had once written and continued to be intrigued with what he was reading. He was confused by the reference to privacy and, in fact, by much of what Jules Smit was saying thus far. But he kept on reading and told himself to expect more confusion.

"How long did you say we'll be staying?, Sylvie asked.

"As long as it takes."

They piled into the car, Paul in the front passenger seat. He indicated they should first check into the Farm Lodge Hotel and from there proceed directly to the Police Service Building.

"For Thatcher Drinkwell?" Jules asked.

"Yes. You know him?"

"A little. Everybody does. Good constable. Even better bird expert. He will tell you about that if you let him."

They swung into a metal railing-lined road, past "Jacob's Ladder" — a seven-hundred-step climb to a fort above — past a bird sanctuary, an elongated tree-fern thicket, stretches of grassland, rows of sunflowers and an occasional foreshortened redwood. The warm damp air became cooler once Jules veered up a steep slope and leveled off on higher ground. Stark contrasts came into view: lush pastures, bare slopes, flax plantations, sea cliffs. Paul stared straight ahead. It had been a long time since he felt so impatient. Still, if he hadn't warned the others about sightseeing, perhaps he would have asked Jules to slow down as they passed some highlights: Ladder Hill, the turtles at the Governor's residence, the Half Tree Hollow neighborhood. Certainly though, there would be later stops at Longwood House where Napoleon lived out his last six years, and his tomb in Geranium Valley.

"The lodge is ten minutes from here," Jules said.

Sylvie and Vincent said nothing. Paul hated to reason why, but he wished the car were not an open convertible. He also wished to talk.

"Do you know the other side here?" he asked Jules.

"How do you mean the other side?"

"Your rivals."

"Yes. Very well."

"Oh?"

"Not so well that we work together. We talk sometimes but we have different purposes."

"Are they Dutch?"

"Dutch? Yes, Dutch."

"And you?"

"Dutch."

"Nice country, especially Amsterdam."

"Thank you, but we live here now."

"I see," Paul said. "You mentioned purposes. How are they different?"

Jules cast a brief look back as if to say he would be uncomfortable providing an explanation. "They bring in some girls. Specialize, you know?"

"I suppose. Prostitution?"

"Yes. We like gambling, the numbers, loans. Clean. Also offer protection. Sometimes that is not as clean. But we never murder. The 'Fish Trick'? They do."

"Wait," Paul said. "Let's back up. What's the 'Fish Trick'?"

"That's the name the Saints gave them. The other side. They operate out of a big black truck. The back has a high canvas cover. Sometimes they haul fish. Other times they haul men. Their own men."

Paul paused to digest the news. "I guess I understand," he said. "Is your side then called the 'Red Car'?"

Jules tightened his grip on the wheel as he roared with laughter. "This? No, this is payment for a loan. Two years ago."

"Okay. And you used the word 'murder'. They murder? I mean, ah, the Fish Truck?"

"If they have to. We can tell when they might because their victim is also in trouble with us."

"But you never hire them to do your dirty work, do you?" Paul had decided to take a chance. His collar felt sticky despite the breeze which stiffened as Jules nearly floored the accelerator.

He looked at the other two in the rearview mirror before responding. "Now we go too far, Dr. D'Arneau," he said, "but the answer is no."

Paul wasn't entirely convinced. Why hadn't Sylvie and Vincent chimed in with a question or two? Then he figured out that they had probably heard little of the conversation over the noise of the motor. Just as well.

The Farm Lodge Country House Hotel appeared to Paul a misnomer. A squat two-story wooden structure, it had only five rooms but was surrounded by manicured lawns and tropical gardens. A plaque near the entrance indicated it was built in the late 17th century as a British East India Company planter's house. He read the plaque twice. *There's that company name again!*

A stout phlegmatic woman behind the registration desk said that two rooms were being held for a certain Paul Darmieur.

There was hardly any debate in settling the mix-up in names and within minutes Paul and Vincent were booked into a twin room and Sylvie, a double room. The accommodations were simple, clean and ample enough for what Paul anticipated would be minimal time spent there. “Ready in ten minutes,” he said.

Conversation during the return trip to Jamestown was sparse. Sylvie complained: “There was no time to change,” her voice louder than usual as a chilly stiff wind kicked up. She wore the same green cardigan as when they had disembarked. She crossed her arms tightly against her chest.

“Why do women always cross their arms like that when it gets cold?” Vincent asked in a loud voice.

“I didn’t think you noticed things like that, Vincent, but to answer your question delicately, we have more to cover.”

“Oh,” Vincent replied.

“Oh?” Paul said from the front seat.

– – –

Rick got up after deciding to take a break. Some of what he’d been reading was beginning to do more than tweak his memory. He wondered why. Was it the personalities who were becoming involved? The situations themselves? No matter: long enough break. He returned to the reading.

At 10 a.m. Jules dropped them off at the entrance to the island’s Police Service Building. It was situated on a quiet side road, straddled by a small neat park and an empty lot.

“I’ll be waiting out back,” he said, “but take your time. I have a book to read.”

The outside of the building looked like a one-room schoolhouse in rural New England. Before walking in, Vincent said to Paul, "Sylvie and I will hang back. You do the talking. We'll listen and try to catch the nuances."

"Agreed," Paul said, "yet speak up if you think it's necessary."

Inside, they passed a small library on the left and a smaller-sized utility room on the right. They opened a wide sliding door and walked through.

What they came upon was plain, containing little more than a wooden desk, four wooden straight-backed chairs, a filing cabinet that faced the door and a cramped holding cell. The main room smelled old but scrubbed, antiseptic. An overhead camera seemed out of place as did a red leather chair behind the desk. A simple glance was sufficient to take it all in. From the ticking and clicking in a tiny back room, Paul assumed it held the usual electronic equipment associated with police departments.

A man of average height and weight stood at the filing cabinet, rifling through some folders. He had short brown hair, a fair complexion, sharply defined features and a faded tattoo of a bird on each forearm. Glasses dangled from an eyeglass cord. He wore a print short-sleeved shirt and khaki pants. He didn't notice Paul and the others entering and he stood plumb straight even though his suspenders gave the impression of pulling him down.

Paul faked a cough. "Excuse me," he said meekly. "Constable Drinkwell?"

The man looked up and smiled. "I like that," he said. "Good to hear once in a while. Usually it's just 'Thatch'. But maybe I shouldn't complain about it. I'd hate to hear 'Constable' all the time. Though he spoke rapid-fire, his keen gray eyes seldom blinked. "May I help you?"

"Well my name is Paul D'Arneau, and this is …"

"Paul!" he shouted, giving Paul a firm handshake. "I should have known. I was told you'd be arriving today but I'm so blasted preoccupied. We have these two gangs on my hands. Each side claims the other is too greedy. Nothing big yet. Just smoldering beneath the surface. Through the years, we've had very little crime but we're expecting that to change. Heaven help us. And we're a small operation. Only a handful of officers to scatter around town, and me. That's it. The gangs are at each other's throats and creating all kinds of problems, but that's not your concern. What is, and I congratulate you for it, is that you're here to inquire about Napoleon. You know, I've been constable on Helena for twenty-six years, sometimes busy, sometimes not, sometimes training officers for Ascension Island, sometimes not. And, not once, not *once* has anyone. Oh, they might ask for directions to the museum. His residence here, Longwood House. But that's about it. I should feel honored that you're here, and I am. Now let's see. These are your associates, are they not?"

"Yes," Paul said finally. He introduced them and they shook hands.

"Happy to meet you," Sylvie said.

"Good to happily meet you," Vincent said. The others gave him a bewildered look.

"I mean to say whatever Sylvie said," Vincent added, flustered. "I apologize. I wasn't trying to be funny. It's just that Sylvie and I haven't had a chance to say much recently. We rushed in and out of the Farm Lodge and our voices didn't carry well in the convertible so we stopped talking. Couldn't hear much of anything for that matter."

"Wait a minute," Drinkwell said slowly. "A convertible? A red convertible?"

"Yes," Paul interjected. "Why? Does that mean anything?"

The constable stroked his barely visible mustache. “No, not at all. I thought for a split second, but no, couldn’t be. We have several red convertibles on the island.”

Paul expected him to walk to the window and see Jules waiting in his car, but he didn’t. *Not yet.*

“Anyway,” Drinkwell said,”let’s sit and talk, shall we? You’ve probably heard that I like to talk. But what do people expect? My wife does most of it at home and some days no one drops in here. I should go out to lunch once in a while but I keep bringing in a damned sandwich. For twenty-six years, I still keep track. That means I’ve saved the cost of over six-thousand lunches. Maybe, what, fifteen-thousand dollars? I always say saving money is good for the soul, as long as you use the money wisely. *All* money should be used wisely."

The three sat and Drinkwell, rounding his desk, patted his leather chair. “Take this chair for instance. One of our school groups gave it to me for my twenty-fifth year on the job. Can you believe it? Now why’d they go and do that? Coulda put the money to better use. There isn’t a lot of it around these parts. You certainly know we’re what’s called a British Dependent Territory and as such, two-thirds of our budget comes from the U.K. You’ll never guess where we get a good chunk of the other third. The sale of postage stamps!”

It hadn’t taken Paul long to realize he liked the constable and found himself unwinding. He looked over at a more relaxed Sylvie and Vincent.

Drinkwell reached down to the bottom desk drawer and withdrew a loose-leaf binder. “Let’s see,” he said, putting on his glasses. “I have what I wanted to cover.” He flipped through a few pages. “Yes, here it is. I must confess I’ve been waiting for this opportunity and I’ve made an outline so I wouldn’t miss anything. I also have some quoted passages to read you. They really get to the heart of how Napoleon felt when he got here. So here we go. By the way, how was your voyage?"

"In a word," Paul said, "exhausting."

"Yes, I know. Unfortunately that's one of our rules. Nothing by phone or mail, only in person. The 'rotten rule of the *histarians'* I call it. And when we work with a client, we coordinate our efforts. He referred to the binder again. "Yes, coordination. What that means is I'm aware of what my good friend, Clive Weaver, covered, so for your benefit we eliminate duplication, and for our benefit we have a division of labor. He stared at Paul. "Make sense?" he asked.

"Yeah, real good sense," Paul replied. He removed a note pad from his briefcase and said, "You have your notes." He checked with the other two and saw that they already had pads and pencils poised. "May *we* take notes?"

"Yes, indeed. And referring to others, how's my good friend Leon Cassell? What can I say about him? A wonderful person; very committed. I remember the first time he came to Helena."

"Hold on! Please!" Paul exclaimed. "He's *been* here?"

"Why yes, twice that I know of. Once for business; once for pleasure. At least that's what he said at the time. Is it a surprise?"

"No, not at all. I must have him confused with another of my Parisian friends."

Paul had to fumble with his note pad to keep his composure. That and asking Sylvie if she had a sharper pencil. He noticed Vincent studying his shoes.

What's going on? I asked Leon if he's been to Elba and St. Helena and he said neither, didn't he?

Despite the disconcerting revelation, the last thing Paul wanted to do was spoil the rest of the time with the constable. It was hard flashing Drinkwell a what's-next expression, especially while wishing he had a cracker to munch on.

The constable let it pass. He returned to the binder. "The serious matters, the reason you're here, we'll get to it soon. But I should mention what they invariably say about me: 'Talk, talk, talk. Birds, birds, birds.' I already spent time on talking. Now for the birds and I'll cut it short. Anyone else would not be so lucky. Yesiree, the *Birds of St. Helena.* That's the title of my book. I don't keep the little darlings, I just know about them; made a study of them. Their history, their habits and so forth. So I must dispense with that first."

It was as if he had a compulsion that had to be satisfied, an overture to a symphony. Without consulting his notes, he spoke with authority, and in a deeper voice. "Not many seabirds here. They shun us and I don't know why. There are plenty off Ascension but we only have Tropic Birds and Black and Brown Noddies. Some call the Fairy Tern a seabird. I don't because it nests not only on cliffs but also in trees and on some of our buildings. You may spot some. They're interesting birds with translucent wings and eyes that seem too big for their heads. As for land birds, most seem to fly around Jamestown primarily. I maintain they're social creatures. They like to be around people. We have ten species here, only ten in all, like Waxbills, the Common Myna, the Malagasy Fody, and Swainson's Canary. But my favorite is the Wirebird: Can't miss it; prefers to live on a ridge above Longwood House, but some come down and race around the grounds. They have long spindly legs and no way will you catch one. They're too quick and fast. They'd rather run than fly. I would have named them Ground Wirebirds."

Drinkwell stopped. “You know,” he said, “I should have offered you some coffee or tea. Would you like a cup?”

All three shook their heads no. “I thought of coffee,” he said, “because I was afraid I might’a been putting you to sleep.”

“No, no, not at all,” Paul said. “It’s very interesting. Migration and all that.”

“Well, I didn’t get into migration or more important, when and how certain birds were released here and decided to stay, and don’t worry, I won’t. In fact, that’s enough on that. It’s putting *me* to sleep!”

He turned the page and unclipped a smaller piece of paper. “Next, the quoted material. The only reason I want to read it is that I never had it printed out or I’d give you a copy. It’s in my longhand hieroglyphic scrawl. And the reason I’d like you to hear it is because it creates a mood and, what should I call it? A poignant picture of one of the great personalities in history. Forgive me if I sound biased, and certainly you, Paul, know the character of the man you’ve scrutinized, but to assist in this mission of yours, perhaps this might explain why the emperor believed as he did. Not in wars, mind you, but off the battlefield.”

Paul’s attentive demeanor matched that of Sylvie and Vincent. Spellbound? The constable took a deep breath, stood at attention and began:

I took this account from the diary of Comte de Las Cases. He was in the small entourage that accompanied Napoleon in exile. The Comte wrote:

‘We were all assembled around the emperor, and he was recapitulating these facts with warmth’:

> For what infamous treatment are we reserved? This is the anguish of death. To injustice and violence they

> now add insult and protracted torment. If I were so hateful to them, why did they not get rid of me? A few musket balls in my heart or my head would have done the business, and there would at least have been some energy in the crime. Were it not for you, and above all for your wives, I would receive nothing from them but the pay of a private soldier. How can the monarchs of Europe permit the sacred character of sovereignty to be violated in my person? Do they not see that they are, with their own hands, working their own destruction at St. Helena? I entered their capitols victorious and, had I cherished such sentiments, what would have become of them? They styled me their brother, and I had become so by the choice of the people, the sanction of victory, the character of religion, and the alliances of their policy and blood. Do they imagine that the good sense of nations is blind to their conduct? And what do they expect from it? At all events, make your complaints, gentlemen; let indignant Europe hear them. Complaints from me would be beneath my dignity and character; I must either commend or be silent.

Drinkwell slowly removed his glasses and let them drop to his chest. "Powerful," he said. "At least I think so. He was certainly controversial but I admired the man. I felt sorry for him … the way he ended up … though many other people didn't. Not at all. Oh well, let's proceed. I've editorialized and given you my pet stuff long enough. Thank you for your patience."

Paul, anxious to comment, responded: "But I thank you, and I'm sure Sylvie and Vincent do also." They smiled their approval.

"You're very kind. Kinder than some of the demanding researchers who occasionally pop in: the mariners, the astronomers, the weathermen."

The constable put on his glasses again and searched through his notes. "With your permission , Paul, I propose to give you some background and related facts as we've been able to assemble them, then offer you my interpretation. You can take it from there and hopefully piece it all together. So just to be sure we're on the same page, we're trying to establish whether Napoleon died a natural death or whether he was murdered or whether it was suicide. Right?

"Right," Paul replied, "and if he was murdered, who did it?"

"Okay. I have much to say about it. It's all outlined here in my binder. I've actually rehearsed the things I want to say to you, but interrupt me if things don't seem clear. Paul had the feeling there wouldn't be any need for interruptions.

"And expect to hear the same language others have used in describing things because we've conferred on them so often lately. You've spoken to most of them."

"Who?"

"The prior, Clive weaver, Leon Cassell, other histarians you haven't met. Middle management so to speak. They do much of the legwork, the endless confirmation work."

"Perhaps I'll meet some other histarians before it's all over."

"Perhaps. It depends on how far along you get. Now first off, the poisoning thing. I know that some feel Napoleon was fed arsenic from 1812 on; that they wanted it to be a slow death so he would fail in his battles. And when he didn't die that way, they finished the job here on Helena. I'll return to that in a minute. My thoughts on hair samples with high concentrations of arsenic. And the silly idea that it came from dye in the wallpaper at

Longwood? Nonsense. In my opinion, there's no final proof the samples were his, and if the wallpaper did him in, why didn't it happen to anyone else who lived there?"

"But the bottom line is that you do believe he was being poisoned?" Paul asked.

"No doubt about it."

"Enough to kill him?"

"That's different. I can't say definitely. No doubt you know who Montholan and Lowe were."

"Yeah. Montholon was his aide-de-camp and Hudson Lowe was governor of the island. He and Napoleon despised each other."

"Maybe those two guys gave him a big swig of arsenic near the end. Or maybe they just saw to it that he received no more of it."

"Come again?"

"I knew you'd ask, so I brought along a statement one of our histarians sent me from Romania. I hope I'm not overwhelming you with all of this." Drinkwell removed a card from the top drawer of his desk and read from it:

> In Europe, arsenic was used by some as a mind-altering drug. In small doses it produced a feeling of well-being and strength. When a man has once begun to indulge in it, he must continue to indulge or the last dose kills him. Indeed the arsenic eater must not only continue his indulgence, he must also increase the quantity of the drug, so it is extraordinarily difficult to stop the habit; for, as the sudden cessation causes death, the gradual cessation produces such a terrible heart,

> knowing that it may probably be said that no genuine arsenic eater ever ceased to eat arsenic while life lasted.

The phone rang. “Excuse me,” Drinkwell said, picking up the receiver. “Yes? No, tomorrow. Well, have it your own way then. Later today. Bye.”

His face showed no emotion although he shook his head from side to side. “Sorry for the interruption but I’m a one-person operation in here.” He scanned his notes. “Alright, you ready for more?”

“Yeah, you’re on a roll, Thatcher.” Paul had eased up on formality but he couldn’t bring himself to call the man, “Thatch”.

“Now we have the critical issue of Lady Ashley Beckett. Not many people know about her and her carryings-on, and I’m aware of others briefing you on her. So there’ll be some overlap here, some repetition. But that’s okay because it’s a rather complicated tale. She was an English lady who, as you Americans would say, had the 'hots’ for Napoleon, so much so that for many years, she followed him, stalked him, stayed with him, whatever. Not that he resisted. Especially when he occupied Longwood. He would welcome her there. It’s reported that she would stoop to anything just to be near him; even bothered him when he was in battle; would buy her way with cash or sex to get to him. Now the ever-present Talleyrand fits into the picture. Some of his family helped her see Napoleon here on Helena. They and no doubt Talleyrand himself received the same things in exchange.”

Sylvie uncrossed her leg and craned forward. “When did you say Lady Beckett took up with him?”

“Probably around 1814, near the end of the campaign in France. For the record, that followed the humiliating Russian campaign a year or so before. Napoleon lost badly in France.

Paris had been besieged; he abdicated for the first time; said goodbye to the Old Guard at the Château of Fontainebleau; and was banished to Elba. That about right, Paul?"

"On the money."

"I love your American expressions!"

The constable poured himself a glass of water from a silver decanter. "Want some?" he asked the others. They said no in unison and appeared happy for the break, for a chance to bring their notes up to date. After draining the glass, he said, "Hope I'm not going too fast," but he didn't wait for a response.

"Carrying on then, two important points must be included in the Lady Beckett story. One is that she had an illegitimate child, a girl, most definitely by Napoleon. We've traced her lineage to a woman who lives in Brussels. We can have our histarian there arrange for you to meet with you if you wish."

"We'll see," Paul said.

"And two, that she was one of the top executives with the East India Company. I'm sure that all three of you are familiar with that company: tea and spices; long sea journeys from England to India and back; stopovers at islands including here. Now bear with me." He examined his notes carefully. "During our extensive research, the names of five men surfaced over and over again. They all worked for the East India Company. They presumably answered to Lady Beckett and there were two other men who may have played key roles in stealing Napoleon's body. But we'll get to that in a second. For now, let's say we have definite proof that these last two were paid handsomely to assist the other five in whatever schemes they came up with. Helping Lady Beckett penetrate this heavily guarded island in order to see Napoleon? Stealing his body and replacing it with someone else? If so, we're not yet sure why. Maybe you can soon find out, but we'll keep trying. Those middle management histarians, remember?"

"That's a key question, isn't it?" Paul asked. "Why steal the body?"

"Yes it is, and as I said, I don't have an answer."

Paul wanted to stay on the subject. "On a related matter, what's your take on the theory that Napoleon isn't in the tomb at Invalides at all, but that a double is in there? Those who propose it claim all sorts of circumstantial evidence, such as, he frequently used impersonators throughout his reign. Some conspiracy buffs even believe he escaped from Helena early in his exile and was replaced by some man in the end stages of stomach cancer. Hardly seems possible but if true, where did Napoleon escape to; when did he die; and where did his body end up?"

Drinkwell sat quietly, rubbing his forehead. Finally he said, "I find it hard to believe he's not in the tomb at Invalides, but there's only one way to find out."

Paul, jolted, looked at Sylvie who looked at Vincent who looked at Paul who stared at Drinkwell before following up with: "I'm sure we have the same thing in mind. Could it ever be done? In a million years?"

Thatcher squirmed in his chair. "Your Leon can arrange *anything*," he said. The number of important friends he has goes, I'd say, beyond the pale. Politicians, heads of state, public officials, military men, curators, educators, media moguls, opinion makers. You name it. Current and former. Inside France, outside France, even in the States. A huge undertaking, but Leon's the man who could pull it off. And I'll let it go at that."

The constable's body language indicated he was uncomfortable with the subject, so Paul didn't pursue it.

"But let me ask a question of my own," Drinkwell said. "Why did Lady Beckett inherit the most money in Napoleon's will?"

"Because she made him happy," Paul responded.

"C'mon Paul, and I say this with all due respect. Not to Napoleon but to you. Many women made him happy. Two he married, others were mistresses, and they were all over the map: Josephine, Marie Louise, Désirée, Pauline, Marie Walewska, Mademoiselle Georges, Giuseppina Grassini, Madame de Stael. He liked to flaunt his mistresses." Drinkwell quickly found a quote in the binder. "In fact he once said, 'I am not a man like others and moral laws or the laws that govern conventional behavior do not apply to me. My mistresses do not in the least engage my feeling. Power is my mistress.'

"But he wrote love letters to all of them and each one sounded more convincing than the others." Again the constable went to his binder. "Here are samples to four of them. You may find them interesting, and they'll give you a flavor of other things on his mind."

Paul had read many of Napoleon's love letters before; nonetheless he accepted the samples and inserted them in the envelope in his briefcase.

"So I say," the constable continued, "we'll probably never know why Lady Beckett ended up with the largest inheritance. But speaking of the will brings me to my last point, and I know you'll want an answer and it's very simple: I don't know. The question is where's the amendment to the codicil? None of us has any idea. The prior talks about a 'decision' and a 'plan hatched on Elba.' We now know the decision was Lady Beckett's inheritance, but the plan? The prior seems to think it's what the amendment's all about. I can't begin to guess. And just in case you're wondering, Clive Weaver told me he gave you a copy of Napoleon's will and its codicil. Which I was told refers to, but doesn't include, an amendment. To date, then, we have three questions with no answers: why would anyone want to steal the body, if that actually happened in the first place? Where's the amendment? And the big one: did he die of natural causes like stomach cancer or was he killed by arsenic or otherwise? Correct?"

"Correct, but with all due respect, the shoe's on the other foot now. Really, with all due respect, Thatcher, you keep forgetting. If he didn't die a natural death, or an accidental arsenic death, who was the murderer?"

A uniformed officer rushed in and, after spending a few moments in the back room, rushed out muttering :"Forgot my flask."

"Tea, not whiskey," Drinkwell said.

Paul seemed oblivious to the intrusion. "Another question," he said. "What did Napoleon do with most of his time here besides what we've all read about? You know, like walking, gardening, billiards, cards, chess, dictating memoirs?"

"Well," the constable said,"for the conqueror of most of Europe, nearly six years in captivity must have been pure hell. He was miserable, became melancholic and didn't do much more than what you listed. He apparently sat a lot, staring off into space. The prior believes he was turning schizophrenic even before he abdicated. And there are some hints that as time wore on, he began suffering from a kind of paranoia."

Drinkwell opened yet another drawer and brought out a second binder. "I have a collection of entries to his diary, word-for-word. I'd like to read a couple to you. Takes a while but I think worth it, to shed light on his mental state and even, when he talks about his conquests, to get a sense of the enormity of it all.

Of course, keep in mind that it's hard to tell when changes in his mental status began: during his last military defeats or once he was settled here.

"I penciled in asterisks for the two I'd like to read." He rifled through several sheets of paper. First we have *'A questa casa. O in questo luogo tristo, non voglio niente di lu'"*

I hate this Longwood. The sight of it makes me melancholy. Let him put me in some place where there is shade, verdure, and water. Here it either blows a furious wind, loaded with rain and fog. *che mi, taglia, l'anima; or if that is wanting, il sole mi, brucia, il, cervello*, through the want of shade when I go out.

"His use of Italian rather than French; is it a sign of abnormal regression. Back to his childhood?

"As for the second entry, I'm no psychiatrist but it strikes me as weird. You be the judge":

> Man loves the supernatural. He meets deception halfway. The fact is that everything about us is a miracle. Strictly speaking, there are no phenomena: my existence is a phenomenon; this log that is being put in the chimney is a phenomenon; my intelligence, my faculties, are phenomena; for they all exist, yet we cannot define them. I leave you here, and I am in Paris, entering the Opera; I bow to the spectators, I hear the acclimations, I see the actors, I hear the music. Now if I can span the space from St. Helena, why not that of the centuries? Why should I not see the future like the past?

> Would the one be more extraordinary, more marvelous than the other? No, but in fact it is not so.

The constable was breathing as though he'd just finished a foot race. He swallowed a half glass of water without stopping. "So those are the questions, " he said, "some answered, most not. Sometimes even digging out the important questions is progress. And there are probably more than we even know about."

Vincent straightened while saying, " So we keep coming back to the same questions."

"Yes, and to repeat myself, they'll probably generate others as you think about them."

Vincent forced his lips into a smile and said, "I have one that's not really related and it's a bold one, Constable, but only if you take it the wrong way. May I ask it?"

"By all means. Nothing's too bold in this business."

"How do you know so much about Napoleon? I mean, you have extensive notes you keep referring to.

"Vincent, I've made a study of him. As I've said, I admire him, despite his greed, his bravado, even his mental collapse. And I'm not even sure about that. There can often be a fine line between brilliance and insanity. I'm happier believing he was brilliant but I can't discount madness."

And while Paul's mind was in overdrive, Sylvie chimed in, "Let's not forget he was also the Father of Sexism."

Paul had to stand and stretch. "Thatcher," he said, massaging his upper arm, "you may or may not know about my new manuscript and that I included Talleyrand as a suspect in Napoleon's possible murder."

"Yes indeed. Got you suspended from Yale I heard."

Paul shrugged and held out his arms in a gesture of helplessness. “I have no secrets anymore,” he said. “You guys really communicate.”

“The constable’s eyes narrowed as he shook his head smugly.

“Well,” Paul said, “what’s *your* opinion?”

“Talleyrand as a murderer?”

“Uh-huh.”

“Honest answer?”

“Honest answer.”

“No.”

“That’s what I thought you’d say and just to be accurate, I wasn’t suspended. I was fired.”

Vincent looked as though he had another question for Drinkwell. He raised his hand this time.

“Another bold one?” Vincent asked.

“As many as you want.”

“Why did you become an histarian? There’s no apparent financial reward. No public acclaim. No increased social status.”

The constable leaned back and clasped his hands behind his head. “Ah, but there other rewards. More important ones. And these apply not only to me but to my colleagues as well, all over the world. I know because we’ve talked about them. It’s remarkable how some motivations can be the same in different countries, among different people. And what are these rewards, these motivations? To know you’re helping in worthy causes. We’d never take a project that was dishonorable. To satisfy historical curiosity. To be like a mountain climber who climbs simply because the mountain's there. Or like the sculptor whose work in mediocre, yet stays with his craft because he considers it art for art's sake." He transferred his hands to the top of the desk and with his eyes drifting over his three visitors, said softly,"And that's why we're histarians."

Paul rose. "On that note we'd better be going. We can't thank you enough, Thatcher, for your time and all the information you've given us. I hope we can return the favor someday."

"It's been my pleasure. I only wish you didn't have to pay the price of listening to my bird lecture!"

At the sliding door, Paul said, "Thanks again and if you ever come to the States, do look me up. Come to think of it, I totally forgot to suggest the same to the prior and Clive Weaver. Will you tell them for me?"

"I'd be glad to. Maybe we'll make the trip together. Who knows?"

Paul slid the door shut and Vincent said, "Bright fellow."

"Self-taught I would assume," Paul said.

"From the looks of it," Sylvie kicked in, "he must have plenty of time to read while on the job. He's got that library there."

Paul seemed to be in no hurry to leave the building and his walking became more of a shuffle. He was vastly disturbed over learning about Napoleon's possible loss of mental faculties, over some indication of insanity.

When they were directly opposite the library, this insanity business harkened him back to a case closer to home, one he'd wondered about for many years. "Wait," he said, leading the other two into the library. "I hope the book I'm thinking about is in here: *Famous Crimes Revisited.*

It didn't take long to find it and once he did, he asked the others if they would mind if he sat at a table while he read through a case about Charles Lindbergh.

"It's a fascinating story, except for the ending. You can make yourself comfortable in the chairs over there near the magazines."

The others nodded and Vincent said, "No problem, Paul, Take your time. But what's with Lindy?"

"I think he went nuts, too. I don't know exactly why but this Napoleon outcome brought it all back to me. It's like two big-time heroes turning whackado. I think about it every so often so I'd like to skim through the section and refresh my memory."

Rick took time to ponder:

So now I'll be reading within what I ***was*** *reading. A reading within a reading. Can get confusing.*

At the table, Paul began:

> "The time was May20-21, 1927. Twenty-five-year-old Charles A. Lindbergh flew a monoplane, the *Spirit of St. Louis*, from Roosevelt Field, Long Island, New York, to the LeBourget Airdrome outside Paris. He was the first person to fly the Atlantic Ocean alone, covering a distance of 3,735 miles in 33 hours, 39 minutes. He burst onto the international scene as a genuine hero, was made Colonel by the U.S. Secretary of War and received the Congressional Medal of Honor and the Distinguished Flying Cross. At the request of the U.S. government, he traveled widely as a special goodwill ambassador and, on a trip to Mexico, he met Anne

Spencer Morrow, the daughter of the American ambassador there. They married two years later. Subsequently he taught her to fly and, together, they embarked on numerous flying expeditions around the world, charting new travel routes for several airlines. But Anne's first love centered on writing, and in the following years, she received critical acclaim for her poetry, memoirs and novels.

To escape media attention, the Lindberghs built a home on a remote 400-acre tract of land near Hopewell, New Jersey. There, on the rainy Tuesday night of March 1, 1932, their 20-month-old son was kidnapped from his nursery. Within hours, an unorganized horde of police and press personnel swarmed over the grounds and by morning, scores of curious onlookers had joined them.

The child's disappearance was detected at 10 p.m., the police were called at 10:25 and at midnight, H. Norman Schwarzkopf of the New Jersey State Police, arrived to take command (He was the father of the 1991 Desert Storm commander). But much of his authority was usurped by Lindbergh, since the hero in effect took charge of the investigation.

In the wet ground directly below a second-story window to the nursery, the police discovered shallow footprints but neglected to measure them, photograph their sole pattern or cast them with plaster. Sadly lacking also were measurements and photographs of apparent footprints found inside the nursery.

A homemade ladder lay flat on the ground, 70 feet from the house. It was built in three sections with the top section lying 10 feet away from the other two. A ¾-inch chisel was also found nearby.

Two holes were located in the clay beneath the window, and one of the troopers immediately fit the ladder into these impressions without first checking for trace evidence at the leg ends of the ladder. Nor had the holes been examined, measured or cast for future comparisons.

Over the next few days, authorities believed that the theft was the work of more than one person, possibly a gang; and three possibilities emerged:

1. Lindbergh believed the kidnappers were professional.
2. Schwarzkopf thought the criminals were local and unprofessional because of their familiarity with the house and the location of the nursery window with its broken shutter latch.
3. Other investigators believed domestic employees were involved because somehow the kidnappers knew that, because the child had a cold, the family had decided against their custom of returning Monday mornings to Anne's parents' estate in Englewood, New Jersey.

On May 12, the child's badly decomposed body was discovered only four miles from the Hopewell mansion. He was face downward and covered with leaves and insects. Less than 24 hours later or 73 days after the kidnapping, the remains of Charles A. Lindbergh, Jr. were cremated.

Before that, what many called a "rinky-dink" autopsy had been performed, because the county physician had suffered an arthritis flare-up and delegated a funeral home director to make the actual dissections. Examination of the skull revealed four fracture lines and a decomposed blood clot. No photographs of this pathology were taken.

Other than the boy's remains prior to cremation, the principal pieces of evidence at that point were the ladder, the chisel, a hard-to-decipher letter from the kidnapper(s), and a modest ransom demand. There were no fingerprints or useful footprints. The ladder would later prove to be crucial.

Early isolated spottings of the ransom bills were made in New York City but such detection escalated when, in the spring of 1933, President Franklin Roosevelt ordered all gold certificates to be exchanged at Federal Reserve Banks, thus taking the country off the gold standard. None of the sightings could be traced. And then, a major breakthrough occurred in September, 1934 when a dark blue Dodge sedan appeared at a gas station in Manhattan and the driver paid for gas with a $10 gold certificate which was on the ransom list. The attendant wrote the license number of the car on the bill which was eventually traced to a Bronx resident, Bruno Richard Hauptmann. He was arrested the following morning.

The ladder was viewed as controversial. It was crudely constructed but *Hauptmann was a professional carpenter.*

During the ensuing trial, a piece of prosecution evidence was the connection of a section of floorboard from Hauptmann's attic to the ladder used by the kidnapper(s). The defense argued that not only was the placement in the ladder's rail disputable but also that such evidence could have been planted.

The argument and the theory! Is history always repeating itself? Why wasn't the defense team ever allowed to inspect the attic?

Another issue concerned handwriting. The State's array of handwriting experts overwhelmed the defense's feeble two. But more recently, document examiners for the U.S. Secret Service and for the U.S. Army concluded that Hauptmann **did not** write the ransom notes.

Throughout the trial, as estimated 100,000 people filed into Flemington each day. After hearing 29 days of testimony, the jury retired for deliberations and returned 12 hours later with a verdict of guilty. Arguing his innocence to the end, Bruno Richard Hauptmann was electrocuted on April 3, 1936.

As a postscript to all of this, his execution had been preceded by a year of legal appeals, and late in that process, sentiment about Lindbergh began to change. Remarkably, as the public turned more and more against the one-time international hero, doubts about Hauptmann's guilt arose across the country. The positions of the two became reversed for reasons that involved, among others, the public's perception of the prosecution team and Lindbergh's decision to abandon his homeland. He sailed for England in late 1935 with his wife and second son and lived there and on an island off the coast of France for more than three years.

> In the immediate post-trial months, those players important to the prosecution became transformed into unattractive personalities in the eyes of the media, principally because they were suddenly viewed as persecutors and self-promotors. Lindbergh, meanwhile, operated from his base in Europe and entered into an intense and open relationship with Nazi Germany … this at a time when the Second World War was at hand and American sympathies were being scrutinized. He made frequent trips to Germany, announced his admiration for the German Luftwaffe, and befriended its leader, Hermann Goering.
>
> At home, many people labeled Lindbergh a dupe of German propaganda, a fascist, even a Nazi, and after the war was begun, he was considered an unpatriotic appeaser.

Rick took a moment to ponder: *What's the lesson to be learned about Lindy and Napoleon? Is it: don't become too much of a hero or you'll go crazy?*

Chapter 26

Rick resumed his reading, trying not to be confused by the stop-off at the library:

Paul, Vincent and Sylvie were approaching the red convertible and all three froze! The car was parked against a chain link fence that surrounded the parking area. The door was open on the driver's side.. Jules Smit's body was half in, half out of the car, his upper body slumped awkwardly across the seat, his legs touching the ground.

Paul felt as though the air had been sucked out of his lungs but he managed to lean down and withdraw the Heritage 9 mm from his ankle rig. Vincent said nothing as he yanked out his Beretta .45. Each held his pistol with both hands as the three inched forward.

"Stay close behind us, Syl," Paul whispered.

At the car, he bent over the body and saw an apparent bullet wound on the side of Jules's head. A trickle of blood was caked down to his shoulders. There were no signs of life.

When they rushed back to inform the constable of their discovery, he pounded the desk with his fist and exclaimed, "Damn it! I knew it. I knew it would happen sooner or later. Now what? Retaliation by his friends?" He stood, walked over and put his arm on Paul's shoulder. "I'm so sorry you had to find the body," he said.

"Do you think it's a signal for us to stop what we're doing?" Paul asked innocently.

"Good point," Drinkwell said. "I never gave that a thought. But who would go this far?"

Paul didn't want to elaborate.

"Just in case though," Drinkwell added, "I'm giving you police protection while you're on the island."

"But Thatcher, there's no need for …"

"Nonsense. I insist and I'm in charge, right?" He gave a thin smile and jabbed Paul's side with his elbow. "Now let's go out and check on the body, process the scene. Then I'll have to make some calls and take a brief statement from you, Paul. I apologize but that's the protocol … Christ, I sound like this is an everyday occurrence around here … we have our share of vagrants and swindlers, but not many murderers. By the way, what's the victim's name?"

"Jules Smit."

"*That's* the man, or at least one of them. Active with the 'Pins'."

The 'Pins'?"

"It's what we named them. The other gang's the 'Needles'."

Instead of laughing, Paul said, "So it's pins and needles. Right now, that's about the way I feel. On them." He was hazy about the difference between the "Pins" or the "Needles", and the "Fish Truck" but he let it drop. He had gotten the overall picture.

Drinkwell grabbed a camera, tape measure, and a notepad and led the others out back. In the way, Paul eased to the constable's side and whispered, "One last thing, Thatcher. The ship that Leon spoke to you about … he did, didn't he?"

"Yes. It's docked and ready to go whenever you give the sign. I hope you decide not to and can stay a bit longer."

The phrase "a bit longer" rang in Rick's ears. Once more, he wondered if he should continue with what he had already written so many years ago. I have to remind myself:

They're my own words, but so what? No one's telling me not to, so I'm carrying on. In fact, my words are more interesting now than when I wrote them nearly two decades ago.

"In that connection, is there a value in visiting the grave site or even Longwood?" Paul asked. "I was thinking of it as a sightseeing opportunity but now, under the circumstances, I just wonder."

"In the case of Longwood, who knows? There are documents under glass there and other artifacts. You might be able to decipher some things that no one else has. Even extract a tiny clue. Regarding the gracesite in Geranium Valley … some call it the Valley of the Tomb … I wouldn't imagine there are many clues there now, but it's a lovely experience. Napoleon selected the site himself, you know. Or at the very least you can say to your friends back home that, yes, you saw where Napoleon lived and where he was buried on St. Helena."

But the last thing on Paul's mind was impressing friends. Besides, none of them knew of his secret mission.. One thing that **was** on his mind, however, was what Vincent and Sylvie thought about Drinkwell's overall reactions, his choice of the word "retaliation", and his reference to gangs. Paul decided that with Smit now gone, he would address the issues directly. The constable had moved well ahead.

"You should both know," Paul said, "that Jules implied he had some friends who were members of a gang here. Said he was sympathetic to their cause and that they never resorted to murder."

"From the back seat, we couldn't tune in on your conversation, but I for one got that impression once Drinkwell spoke up," Vincent explained.

"Same here," Sylvie added.

Not only had the constable supplied an officer in a police cruiser to follow the trio, but he also had their rental car arrive within a matter of minutes. This time Paul drove, his hands tight on the wheel, claiming he was more rattled than the other two and that, in a way, it would help calm his nerves. Seldom had he admitted to such weakness as he termed it. He also reflected on the sobriquets "Pins" and "Needles" and "Fish Truck". He hated the sound of them and said so.

"You're entitled to it and I don't blame you," Sylvie said from the passenger seat. "It's really *your* mission and they know it. Whoever 'they' is. Let's pray it's part of the gang violence the constable talked about."

But it was comments about Paul's safety that reflected the most emotion … deep and dolorous. "Must we worry about you, Paul? We had a scare on Elba, and now Helena. What about Paris when we return? Can't we leave here earlier? I'm worried about you, Paul, or did I already say that?" She received no answers and seemed to expect none.

They parked to the side of the hotel and got out of the car. Paul waved thanks to the police officer who had parked near a stone wall below, conspicuously visible from the main road.

As they walked in, Paul said to Sylvie, "I appreciate your concern and I have my own about you."

"Isn't anyone around here concerned about me?" Vincent asked, with an obvious stab at humor. It fell on deaf ears.

"About eating lunch, Syl, I think we should try. Let's ask Miss Cheery Face over there if she can recommend a place. And just for your peace of mind, and yours too, Vincent … yes, we can leave earlier. Thatcher said he's got a ship ready to sail if we decide. I didn't mention it to you. Don't ask why except I didn't really think it would be necessary."

"You've made up your mind then?" Vincent inquired.

"Yeah, and the way to answer you properly is to say I haven't broken my record."

"Meaning?" Sylvie asked.

"Meaning there were two islands to investigate and two islands to get the hell out of!"

Paul could hear the sighs. "We should leave in the morning," he said. "Let's have lunch and later a decent dinner. The policeman will be nearby just like he is now … and then get an early start tomorrow and carry on with business in Paris, or wherever else we have to go."

"Paul," Sylvie said, "you sound more resolute and that's good but please, please be careful."

"Resolute's my middle name. Haven't you heard?"

Ann's place was exactly as the receptionist had described it: quaint, near the pier in Jamestown, in the middle of an expansive garden. It boasted a variety of popular "Saint" dishes such as curry, pumpkin stew, fishcakes, pilau, black pudding and coconut fingers. It was noisy, jammed to capacity and filled with pleasant food aromas. They were told that a corner table would open in a few minutes so they took temporary seats on a leather sofa near the door.

"To answer another of your questions back there, Syl," Paul said, "my heart and brain tell me not to be in the mood, but my stomach's hungry."

Soon they were seated. Paul didn't waste any time. "Any bets on the most burning item we all want to bring up?"

"I'll go first," Vincent said. "Drinkwell's remarks about Napoleon's tomb."

"Ditto," Sylvie said.

"Unanimous," Paul announced. "Think Leon has the wherewithal to set it up … if we decide to go ahead? You're both in a better position to make that judgment then I am."

"No doubt about it," Vincent said. "Whether or not he would do it is another thing though. He may think it's unnecessary. We'd have to make a convincing case for it."

"I agree," Sylvie said. "I think if we can present the reasons for going to all that trouble, he'd cooperate. He wants very much for the mission to succeed and you, Paul, are the … the … pivotal person here. He has great faith in you … you must know that by now."

"I have to admit," Paul said, "in listening to this, you both already favor having a look-see."

"If there's any question about who's there," Vincent said, "we'll have to."

They each ordered fishcakes and black pudding and raced through the meal as though they were late for a job interview.

Back at the hotel when Paul was informed that dinner reservations for St. Helena's finest restaurants had to be made in person, he threw up his hands and almost shouted a word he only used privately, like after the time he accidentally smashed his thumb with a hammer. "We could have made one while we were there!" He stared at Sylvie and Vincent. Finally he said in his most contrived voice, "Ann's Place will do, right? Good food."

They nodded. "And nice atmosphere," Sylvie said.

"I didn't notice," Paul responded. "Look, we'd better make the reservation before we go to Longwood. I'll drive back to town and get it over with."

Giving his name and desired time at the restaurant's reservation counter took all of a minute. As he turned to leave, a young woman holding a portable phone approached him and said, "Are you Paul D'Arneau?"

"Yes?"

She handed him the phone. "It's for you."

"Yes?" he repeated into the phone.

A masculine voice at the other end sounded muffled: "Listen hard, my friend. Leave the island immediately or your pretty girlfriend gets hers. Smit didn't listen. We know she's at the hotel and the cop's with *you*. Understand?" Before the click, Paul heard a trailing hyena laugh.

He hurled the phone onto the counter and burst out the door. "To the hotel! Quick!" he screamed as he ran past the police cruiser. He could hear his heart pounding and feel his legs weaken as he leaped into his car and sped off. The police officer eventually overtook him and led the way, his siren blaring. Paul had no trouble keeping up though his mind churned wildly and his hands felt moist.

He came to a dusty halt at the hotel and, before bolting from the car, he yanked out his Heritage pistol. He outraced the officer to Sylvie's room and banged on the door. "It's me, Paul," he shouted. "Are you there?"

Seconds seemed like minutes before the door opened and Sylvie, wrapped in a white robe, appeared and said, "What's wrong? You're sweating."

He pushed past her into the room and looked around before dropping onto the edge of her bed, barely able to catch his breath.

Vincent appeared in the hallway's open door. "What's all the commotion about? What's going on?"

Paul was wiping the back of his neck with his handkerchief. He related what had happened and asked some key questions.

Sylvie explained she had just taken a shower and was fine. "No, there were no phone calls or unusual noises. No, I never left the room." She went on to say she still believed they were bluffing … using threats to get him off the mission, for whatever reason.

"Really?" Paul said sarcastically. He knew better, but having just experienced a monstrous scare … on her behalf no less … he felt her past point trivialized what to him was a matter of life and death. "And what would you say about the castle incident?"

"You told me they didn't show their guns; that they just kept coming toward you."

"And today's murder?"

"A turf war. Nothing to do with us."

"Your kidnapping?"

"A scare tactic."

"Over what? We've never been connected."

"I know. Too bad."

Paul was in no mood to get into *that*.

"What's your opinion, Vincent?" he asked.

"I think we should take them seriously."

"Paul, still emotionally bruised, thought Vincent was hedging … perhaps for Sylvie's sake. "Whatever," he said. "We leave early in the morning, like at six."

"I thought that decision was a done deal," Sylvie said.

"But I never figured so early; guess I'm just anxious to get going. Or maybe a tiny voice is telling me the bad guys are still sleeping at that hour."

The police officer who had been leaning against the door jamb came to attention and said, "You're leaving us so soon?"

Paul tried to soften a piercing look as he replied, "Officer, you heard it all just now and you know about the murder. I thank you for your help, but wouldn't you leave for a while?"

"I suppose. But what's the murder got to do with *you*?"

"I wish I knew for sure." He also wished he could fathom the subtle change he saw in Sylvie: her sharp views, her demeanor, the tone of her voice. He attributed part of it to her way of bolstering his spirits, but the rest? He had no clue. Since the murder, however, he sensed that she was observing him differently, holding her gaze, eyes haunted, like someone who had more to say but dared not say it.

But Sylvie's disposition aside, Paul wanted to remember St. Helena as a timeless culture, a jewel. And it probably was, yet for less than a day it had turned out to be a treacherous and deadly one.

The two men agreed with Sylvie to reassemble in an hour and they returned to their room. Paul immediately called

Thatcher. Without mentioning the phone call and its aftermath, he indicated they'd like to sail at 6 a.m. The constable assured him the ship would be ready.

At 2:30 when they met outside for their trip to Longwood House, the air was cool and Paul could feel the breeze ruffling his hair. Only Sylvie was dressed appropriately, decked out in a dark brown poncho layered over a lighter brown print skirt and white leggings. Paul and Vincent ran back to their room and returned wearing blue blazers.

They found Longwood overrun by tourists and after pausing to view the magnificent gardens, a small gazebo and the sunken footpaths that Napoleon had ordered to hide him from guards, the police officer obliged Paul by accompanying them inside. By now, Paul and Vincent had developed a kind of sign: Paul would gaze down at his ankle and Vincent would pat the left side of his chest.

Vincent and Sylvie took time examining everything on display while Paul moseyed about but discovered nothing unexpected except the profound smell of dampness. What's more, he wasn't that interested and certainly saw nothing in the way of a clue as Thatcher had put it. The visit simply rekindled the haunting possibility that Napoleon had either been deliberately poisoned or stolen … or both.

Within twenty minutes, Paul said, "Okay, let's clear out. The other two reluctantly followed him to the door. The policeman nudged Paul aside saying, "I'll go out first."

An overcast sky and breezy air did little to accentuate the serene beauty of the Valley of the Tomb. Paul took notice of the brook, the geraniums and especially the trees, many of the originals gracefully bent toward the tomb. Again he remembered his reading and his own writings to recapture the details of Napoleon's funeral at the site on which they now stood. The services were held four days after the emperor's death. Three thousand English soldiers of the twentieth regiment participated. *His enemies! Astounding*! Twenty- four of them had carried the coffin down the path to the gravesite. Yet it was the slab of concrete that intrigued Paul the most as it symbolized in his own mind the bitterness between Napoleon and Governor Lowe. The emperor's associates had requested that the word "Napoleon" be inscribed on the slab but the governor refused, insisting on the word "Bonaparte" instead. As a result, the slab remained unmarked for nineteen years.

They spent less than twenty minutes there. It was not Paul's style but he realized without apology that the visit had been nothing short of perfunctory.

It was about 4 p.m. when they arrived at the hotel. "There, that's over," he said. "Two down, one to go."

"What's the third?" Sylvie asked.

"Dinner." Paul was tired of setting the time for when they should be ready for what. He checked his watch. "Remember," he said, "we're boarding at six. So Vincent, you decide … we eat when? It's now four."

"Five-thirty." Vincent said. "Let's leave here at five."

"Okay by me," Paul said. He turned to Sylvie. "Does that allow enough time for a lady to get ready?"

She didn't respond but her expression said it all.

Once in the room, Paul stated he had two phone calls to make: to Leon in Paris and to Victor in Amsterdam.

"You don't think the time difference amounts to much in either city?" Paul asked.

"No, I don't" Vincent replied.

"And in case you're wondering, you don't have to make yourself scarce."

"It took about fifteen minutes to reach Leon.
My goodness! Paul! What's up? How's it going?"

"It went fairly well," Paul said, "and I use the past tense advisedly. We're still in Helena but we're sailing back at six in the morning. A couple of ugly things happened that I'll get to in a minute, but we learned more than expected, even more than we did on Elba.

"You said 'ugly'? Like what? Are the three of you all right?"

"Yeah, considering. But I *must* get something cleared up. That's a polite way of saying I have a bone to pick with you."

"You heard then." It was a statement, not a question.

"Yes, I heard you visited the island at least twice but you told me you'd never been here. Remember?"

"That's correct and I'm sorry about withholding it from you, Paul, but the truth is I didn't want you to depend on my information. I wanted a completely fresh approach. Clear the board as it were. Then if you needed anything that might fill in the blanks later, I might be of help. Though I doubt it because I never found anything I didn't know in the first place. It was some years ago. I went there for the same purpose as you but the historians were just getting off the ground then, so compared to you I was at a great disadvantage."

"Well, okay, but from now on we stick with … you know … the truth. Like the name of your organization, Vérité?"

"Of course. That was bad judgment on my part and again, I apologize."

Paul said he was satisfied with the explanation, then spent considerable time reviewing, first, the consultation with Victor Frelinghuyens; second, the shooting death Of Jules Smit; and third, the threat on Sylvie's life. "The bottom line is we're ready to scram. On the other hand, as I said, we learned plenty. Thatcher Drinkwell was terrific. Very talented. We think he's wasted on this … this lonely island. What do they call it? An emerald set in bronze? More bronze than emerald, I'd say." He next summoned up what the constable had covered: from arsenic to the notion of Napoleon's body being impersonated or stolen; from Michael Ney to Talleyrand; from Lady Beckett to the British East India Company executives; from her illegitimate child to Napoleon's love letters; from her inheritance to the codicil. But Paul did not mention Drinkwell's reference to opening the tomb at Invalides.

Paul couldn't tell whether or not Leon was taking notes, but he had a gut feeling that he was.

"I knew the constable would prove valuable," Leon said, "so all in all the trip was worth taking?"

"I'd have to say yes … all in all. If it weren't for those two setbacks, we'd probably be staying longer. But no way now."

"Did you happen to take in Plantation House?"

"Where the governors live? No. Hudson Lowe was a son of a bitch I hear, and that alone eliminates him as a murderer or body snatcher, as I see it. He was very much despised and I think if he were guilty of anything so horrendous, he would have been found out a long time ago. The secret wouldn't have held up."

"Good logic, Paul."

Paul was unmoved by the compliment and had said all he wanted to say. The conversation ended with Leon's guarantee that the R.A.F. would be waiting for them on Ascension Island and with a brief exchange that apparently delighted the head of Vérité.

"I can't wait to get going," Paul said.

"To the States?"

"No, to Paris."

"I like to hear that, my friend. Do please consider it your adopted home."

The next call would be less confrontational but more painful.

"Paul, it's you?" Victor had answered the phone at once.

"Yes. We're about to leave St Helena and, Victor, I have bad news. Your contact here, Jules Smit? He was found murdered today."

"Murdered? Oh no? How?"

"Shot in the head. Looks like the work of a rival gang."

"Uh … who found him?" It was obvious Victor didn't know what to say next.

"I did."

"I feel bad about this , Paul. The murder, of course, but for you to find the body, to promise you that you'd be protected, and it just … it just broke down. I feel terrible."

"Don't. It's not your fault. Apparently there are some things going on that are new to the island. We spent some time with their constable and he's completely frustrated."

"Paul, answer me honestly. Two questions: one's easy to ask. The other? Well I hope you don't misunderstand. Did this ruin the trip for you? I mean in terms of the goals you set out with."

"No. Except for the damper it put on the situation, we did fine. And your second question? I think I can guess.

"Could this in any way have anything to do with."

"With me and with my companions snooping around? Could be. Who knows?"

Dinner was not memorable. None of the three ordered a drink and all of them poked at their food. Even their conversation … what there was of it … was "under wraps", for they had invited the police officer to join them.

Halfway through the meal, Paul said to him, "You know, we never got your name."

"Smith. Oliver Smith," the officer responded.

"That's Smith, not Smit, right?"

"Smith, sir. If it was Smit, I'd be off grieving somewhere over the killing."

"Do many Smits live on the island?" Vincent asked.

"He's the only one that does … did."

"Did you know him?" Sylvie asked.

"Only of him. He was with the 'Pins'."

"The other gang's the 'Needles' I understand," Paul said.

"Yes sir."

"Then what's the difference between the, say, the 'Needles' and the 'Fish Truck'?"

"Same thing. But strictly speaking, the 'Fish Truck's' been here forever. Longer than I have and I was born here. And the 'Needles' just joined them. They're not as violent."

Paul took a moment before framing his next question. "So, using your best judgment, do you think it was old guard 'Fish Truck' that was behind the murder?"

"Yes sir, no doubt."

"One last question, officer," Paul said, "and forgive me if I sound like a prosecutor, but do you think the 'Fish Truck' might have been around in Napoleon's day?"

"Most likely."

Chapter 27

The ship was named the *Argos*, a small Greek freighter that hauled roll-on/roll-off vehicles, packaged lumber and containers. It had cabin space for twelve passengers in square units that were surprisingly well furnished and comfortable. Paul had no idea when the ship had docked in James Bay, probably during the night

Nor had he asked, but Thatcher Drinkwell had made good on his promise. They set sail at 6:10 a.m. There were no other passengers on board.

Now, having grown accustomed to the pitching and yawing, Paul had mixed feelings. He wanted desperately to figure out how to fill the next thirty-six hours at sea. And although time was moving slowly, he really didn't mind: the pace on St. Helena had finally caught up to him. He took frequent naps, sat thinking on deck and exchanged stories with the crew. There were no games, lectures or entertainment aboard the *Argos*. The dining area was a continuation of the galley in its metallic composition: steel walls, steel floors, steel tables, steel benches. The food was filling and Sylvie and Vincent, obviously in the same throes of boredom as Paul, drew out their meals to the last morsel. But, as on the voyage south a few days before, none of the three spoke much about the mission: just the positives and negatives thus far and, particularly, what needed to be learned, visited or flushed out. Paul wasn't sure about the other two but he could sense the urgency of these initiatives.

At this point his only concrete activities were to update his summations and organize his satchel. To "sanitize the sickening thing", in his words. He was about to open it when he heard a light tap on his door and Sylvie walked in. She wore blue jeans, a loose pink sweater and no makeup or jewelry.

"It's not what you think, Paul," she said, seeing his expression. "This is different. It'll only take a minute. I couldn't handle any more than that right now."

He pointed toward the chair and she sat down softly. He remained standing, his hands in the pockets of his khakis, wondering what was about to happen, on guard for anything.

Sylvie said, "I've been holding things in and I've decided not to do that anymore. I know this may be unexpected and a bit dramatic but I'm bothered by it and maybe telling you will help."

Her fingers trembled as she fumbled with her watch strap.

"Bothered by what?" he asked.

"You."

"What?"

"And me."

Paul held his hands up in a stop gesture saying, "Now hold it, Sylvie. Is this what I think it is? A new approach?"

She didn't answer the question, instead studied her loafers tapping the floor. She then stammered her way through their mutual experiences since he had called on her at the Institute. And she put a spin on each of their meetings. A romantic spin. Her voice took on a plaintive quality.

"Oh Paul, I'm all confused, but you don't see? I'm afraid I'm, ah, falling in love with you. I know that sounds stupid and I know where I stand. You're taken and I know you'll probably always be taken and there's nothing I can do about it. But that doesn't mean I can't tell you about my feelings. Yesterday, the threat on my life upset me more then I let on. It put those feelings in perspective, and I wanted to share that with you before it's too late. Can you understand?"

Paul remained standing, speechless. He clenched his hands in his pockets.

"And believe me," she continued, "I'm not asking anything of you, and I won't embarrass you. I just wanted you to know. And I'll say it again: maybe this will help me."

Paul crossed over and put his right hand on her right shoulder so he could avoid direct eye contact, afraid he couldn't sustain it.

"Sylvie," he said, much like a father, "first of all, as you've indicated more than once, those threats are just that … threats … meant to scare us away. And second, what you just told me is impossible. I'm flattered, very flattered, but it's impossible. Fond of? Maybe. Attracted to? Maybe. But love? We've known each other a little more than a week.

"That's all it took for Josephine with Napoleon."

She dabbed her eyes with a tissue, pushed herself up, walked to a tiny porthole and stared out. "Yes, you're taken," she said, visibly dispirited, "and I wish you great happiness, but if you ever become … untaken, I'll still be in Paris."

Paul couldn't resist: "You mean like Bogy and Bergman and 'We'll always have Paris'?"

"I wish we did. That at least."

Sylvie turned and faced Paul squarely. "There's more to it, I'm afraid, but I've said enough already. For the sake of the mission, let's pretend this conversation never happened, okay? Over and done. I got it off my chest." On her way out the door she stopped to kiss him on the cheek.

Paul sat on the edge of the bed, perplexed. *Was this all an act*? If so, why? Even if it were, he was concerned about the comment, "There's more to it, I'm afraid." And beyond that, he was curious about how she would conduct herself from now on.

A full five minutes passed before he resigned himself to the fact that there were no clear-cut answers. The episode — he preferred the word 'confession' — was just one more thing to worry about. Yet he was determined not to be sidetracked by Sylvie's behavior. He couldn't afford the drain on his psyche. It helped to compare her admission, real or not, to that of a schoolgirl's. But a schoolgirl was not what Paul wanted at this stage of the investigation. *Maybe she'll step aside? Should I ask her?*

There were things he wanted to tend to: possible summations, reorganizing the satchel, examining what Drinkwell had given him in an envelope. Paul forced himself to concentrate.

He took hold of his satchel as if it contained garbage and emptied its contents onto the bed. It *did* contain garbage. He surveyed the pile in disgust: the envelope, Napoleon's will and love letters — the important things — jumbled in among newspaper clippings, written articles, notes, cards, pencils, pens, paper clips, elastic bands, loose coins, a legal pad and other clutter Plus a small box of saltine crackers.

He stepped back as if on defense, and looked around to see if anyone was observing what had taken place. He wasn't in the mood for "sanitizing" after all, so he slid the envelope and love letters aside and threw everything else back into the satchel.

The overriding issue, however, was not the love letters or the envelope — not even Sylvie's startling disclosure — but his long overdue summations. So much had transpired since his last one that he merely wanted to *list* the highlights, not *interpret* them.

And no new questions; there were enough already. The value of this exercise far outweighed the time it took to formulate. It helped him take stock on any given day, to assess where he was coming from and where he might go. He removed the legal pad and pencil, sat at a small table and vowed to be concise as he recorded all he could remember.

The three passengers had five meals aboard the *Argos*. They saw little of one another on those occasions. At the first meal Sylvie and Vincent handed over and briefly editorialized on their notes. During the others, they dominated the conversation with talk of world history and general scientific matters. Paul got the impression they had conspired to divert his attention away from the mission for a change. But it didn't work. He contributed little more than a disingenuous smile and some idle chatter. Actually Paul was waiting for Sylvie to return to her admission of love for him. But it never happened.

He allowed an hour to pass before knocking on her door.

"Well, this is a switch," she said, ushering him in. She wore the same casual clothes she had worn at dinner … a baggy brown jersey and beige slacks … while Paul, barefoot, tried thried to appear blasé in a blue robe. He had rolled up his sleeves and trouser legs to make it appear as though he wore nothing underneath. He sat on the edge of the bed and gingerly crossed his legs so as not to give the charade away. She pulled over a chair, turned it around and straddled it, resting her arms on the back. She stared at him, smiling but not laughing.

"You're making fun of me," she said.

"No I'm not. I'm just trying to lighten a time when you seem cold as ice." He lowered his sleeves and trouser legs, put on a pair of soft slippers he had brought with him and removed the robe. "Guess it didn't work," he said.

"Good try, but I just don't think it's a laughing matter."

"I totally agree. I didn't intend to belittle things … only to humor you. But are you okay?"

"I'm okay now. I got it off my chest."

"You weren't serious though, were you?"

"Silly fellow," she answered, probing his eyes. "As serious as I could be. What do you think?"

"I can't say. I've been trying to make some sense of it."

She pulled back. "Look, you've got too much on your mind as it is. Let's drop it for now. I said what I had to say, and the Paris thing still stands. I meant it." She cupped her hand over her mouth briefly, then took it away. "You talk serious? That's serious."

Paul did the same thing with his hand before saying, "I guess." He resisted the urge to jump up and hold her close, for no other reason than then to create the right mood for what he was about to say next.

"I realize you may want to leave well enough alone," he began, "but I think this needs to be said on my part. Yes, as you put it yesterday, I'm taken. But … and God, I hope this comes out right … you would have made a great wife. I want you to know that, Syl."

"Would have?"

"Yes."

Sylvie got up stiffly and rubbed her arms in front of her chest. She turned, walked to the door and wheeled around. "Paul," she said, her voice taut. "I said I'm okay. Let's not stir things up."

He stood but remained near the bed. "You're right," he said. Guess I didn't stop to think it through. And as long as I'm screwing things up tonight, I might as well ask. You said before that there's more to it. Is this a good time to elaborate, or is it too touchy a subject?"

Sylvie took a step closer and broadened her stance. "Well, I don't know. I don't know if I should. Under the circumstances — that is, once I realized myself how I felt about you — I definitely planned on telling you. But I needed to get up enough courage first."

"Aw, come on now … how bad can it get?"

"Real bad. You may not like me anymore."

"Try me." Paul felt like crossing his fingers. He sat back down gently, hoping she would explain what was still an enigma to him.

She sighed and let her shoulders drop at the same time. "But there has to be a promise in return," she said.

"Like what?"

"Like keeping this a total secret. If anyone in the delegation gets wind of it, I'm ruined with Vérité. I'd be crushed because I believe in Vérité very, very much … although you might not think so once you hear what I have to say."

"I promise … I swear. If I thought it would help convince you, I'd cut my finger with a knife to draw a little blood."

She walked back to her chair and again straddled it. "Here goes," she said. "You do know I've been a spy for Vérité against the Institute, right?"

"Right."

"Well, the reverse is also true. There, I've admitted it. I've been a double agent … that's the simplest way I can put it."

Paul stared at her. "You mean you were spying on Vérité on behalf of the Institute?"

"Not really spying. Helping them. And this is the hard part, Paul. Forgive me. If you have it in your heart, please forgive me. I was helping them dissuade you, to get you off the case. But I was in a bind. In a way, I had no choice. It was either that or …" Her words were tumbling out.

"Wait, wait!" Let's back up. Two questions here. No choice … why? Dissuade me …why?"

"I had no choice because they would have fired me."

"But why did they want me off the case?"

"The Talleyrands."

"Who?"

"You know about him, Paul. Everybody who writes history does." Sylvie waited for a response.

But Paul was too astonished to give one. He scratched his finger. "The Talleyrands? I can't believe it. How did they come into the picture?"

"It's a long story but I'll condense it. You see, I've rehearsed this, figuring I'd tell you some day; not now though. But the same thing with how I feel about you. I didn't want to tell you so soon. They go together, Paul. If I love you, and I do, and if I want to tell you, and I do, how can I not level with you now? Does that make sense? It does to me."

"Yes, it does. Don't worry about it. Please get to the Talleyrands."

"In the late 1790's, Talleyrand was deported from France. I won't go into why and he fled to your country. He was allowed back two years later. The Institute of France was just beginning at the time and it was struggling real bad. Somehow, he came to its rescue. The upshot of it all is that from then on he developed strong ties with the Institute and all its branches, including the one I work for, the Academy of Sciences. This has carried on for years and years so that his present day relatives have terrific pull with the Institute. And they're upset that I named Talleyrand as a suspect in Napoleon's murder. Sound correct?"

"Yes, that is, the *theory* of murder. But how did they know that? It's in my unpublished manuscript."

"That's where Yale comes in."

"Yale?"

"Oh yes … this gets more intriguing by the minute. You won't believe how many things we've been dealing with are all tied together like a ball of, what, string? We've got Elihu Yale, the East India Company, Lady Beckett, and spices to cover yet."

"Now I'm confused. *Really* confused. What the hell do spices and the guy Yale was named after have to do with it?"

"You'll see, but let me finish with the murder theory. The Talleyrands are afraid you might come to a definite conclusion that Napoleon was murdered. They want the public to think it was a natural death and have been pushing that for years. Unnatural death equals an ancestor as a possible killer. Natural death? They forget about the ancestor as a killer."

"But why didn't you tell me about this sooner?"

"Because I was caught in the middle. My job was at stake, but when I saw what they were doing to scare you away, and how much my feeling for you was growing, I thought enough is enough."

"So it was his relatives who were behind the, let's call them, 'incidents'?"

"Yes, all of them."

"Would they have resorted to murder?"

"I don't think so on their own, but once the Mafia comes in, who knows? Signals could get crossed or the hoodlums could get careless."

"What about your kidnapping?"

"A complete hoax. Again, to put a damper on the mission."

Paul sprung up, paced between the bed and door several times and sat back down. "Boy, that had me fooled, all of us. What I don't understand though is how did the Talleyrands know I was in on the case?"

"I told them."

"But"

"It was part of what I had to do at the time."

"Okay, understood. Now, Elihu Yale and spices?"

"Talk about irony! Your former employer and alma mater, right? You indicated it was named after this Elihu Yale fellow. I take it he was the college's largest benefactor, but he was also an official with the British East India Company. Well, Talleyrand was not only a great statesman but also a renowned gourmet and wine connoisseur. He once owned the fancy Châteaux Haut-Brion and hired the best tea and spices from Yale's East India Company. That's how Talleyrand and lady Beckett happened to strike up their friendship and develop the 'covers' used for her to see Napoleon. And all the rest."

"So Yale and the Talleyrand clan are close?"

"Hand and glove, even to this day. And that's how the clan knew about what's in your manuscript. Ahead of anyone else. Then they read who you put at the top of your suspect list, I bet the Yale people contacted them on the spot. In fact, I've got to believe that's why you were let go. For *that* more than for the mythology excuse."

Paul got up again and walked slowly to Sylvie's side. He held out both arms at the same time she began to cry. She took his hands and he gently helped her up.

Now in his arms she said, sniffling, "I wish I didn't have to tell you all that, Paul, but I care about you terribly and you deserve to know."

He kissed her on the forehead and said, "You're a brave woman and I won't breathe a word about it to a soul. You can bank on it."

She pulled away and raised her chin. "But one thing you *don't* deserve," she said, "Is listening to some sniveling French broad who can't control her emotions. You're engaged for heaven's sake!"

For the duration of the trip back to Paris, Paul couldn't dismiss Sylvie's revelations from his mind. Only the arranged encounter with Leon, who was waiting at the de Gaulle Junior airstrip, interrupted his stream of consciousness: from her complicated dual role, to Talleyrand, to Elihu Yale, to the British East India Company, to exotic spices, to Lady Beckett, to trysts with Napoleon, and back to Sylvie. He had paused to dissect each issue, over and over.

What to do? For now, file it away along with everything else in his head.

PART FOUR

Chapter 28

Sunday, May 28
7:40 p.m.

"Getting to be a habit, folks," Leon said.

"Good to see you, Leon," Paul said, "and good to be back."

As before, Sylvie and Vincent walked ahead into the only building at the airstrip. Leon tugged on Paul's jacket and gestured for him to stay behind.

"So the trip was worth it despite those two unfortunate incidents?" Leon asked.

"Definitely. A bit scary and a bit distracting, but not enough to wipe out what we learned. I'm happy we went, but even happier it's over."

"Drinkwell's already called me, filled me in on everything. He thinks you're topnotch, by the way." He didn't give Paul a chance to respond. "So what's next?"

In contrast to the weather in Paris upon their return from Elba, the night was still and balmy. Paul removed his traveling windbreaker and slung it over his shoulder. He had Leon hold his briefcase while he did so.

"This thing weighs a ton," Leon said, handing it back. Again he didn't give Paul a chance to respond, instead answering his own question. "Next I would guess is Belgium?"

Paul gave him a quizzical look.

"I told you Drinkwell filled me in," Leon said apologetically.

"Well, you happen to be right. I want to check out the 'lineage woman', for want of a better name. The constable said she's a direct descendant of Lady Beckett and Napoleon. She may have some important things to say. Plus I may want a DNA sample if she's willing."

"Come again?"

"A DNA sample. I'll explain in due course. Later. Some other things have to crystallize first. Just trust me for now."

It was Paul's first hint that he intended to prove Napoleon had a living relative, and he realized that if Leon considered the logic, the emperor's DNA would also have to be obtained. In addition, if the decision were made to see who occupied the tomb at Invalides—Napoleon or an imposter—and if in either case the body were unrecognizable, its DNA must be extracted. He wondered if Leon would comment. He didn't. Perhaps because he appeared eager to pass on more of what he'd learned from Drinkwell.

"The name of the 'lineage woman'", Leon said. "is Sophie Bauer. She's well liked in the Brussels area. Retired school teacher. Spinster. Nearly everyone around knows of her possible link to Napoleon, even that she may be a descendant of an illegitimate child of his. She's apparently reluctant to talk about it; refers to the child as her unofficial forebear. And there was no mention of a Lady Beckett."

Paul took out his note pad and abbreviated the information. "How did the good constable know all this?"

"He called the *histarian* in the region, actually right there in Brussels, and simply inquired."

"I see. So she *does* exist. Well, can you set up an appointment with her for me? We'll take the Bullet there in the morning. I'll ask Sylvie to come. With her background, she's no doubt had plenty of experience taking buccal smears for DNA."

"Glad to and I'll call you later to confirm it. In the meantime you'd better consider having Vincent go along too. He can wait in the taxi if you'd prefer."

Chapter 29

It was just after 8 p.m. Sunday when Paul arrived at his room at the Meridien Montparnasse. He felt as though he had just come home from a war. A war that was still raging. Even before unpacking he called Jean and spent some initial time talking about how she felt and what was happening at her end. He then launched into a detailed report of the *St. Helena Phase* of the investigation and his latest conversation with Leon. When he got to the Jules Smit murder, it didn't appear to bother her. Either that or she didn't want to show it. Paul next explained why it might become necessary to open Napoleon's tomb and acquire a DNA sample from his remains. Similarly he was planning a visit to a descendant of Napoleon's alleged daughter for a sample of her DNA to confirm the emperor's identity.

"Now review with me, Jean. You gave me a rundown once but I can't keep the DNA's straight. You were talking about tracing someone's ancestry. And no fancy terms."

"You mean nuclear DNA and mitochondrial DNA? They're both used to identify people. Mitochondrial doesn't degrade as easily as nuclear, so it's better for those who died hundreds of years ago. The only problem is that it's passed on from generation to generation only in the female line of the family. You told me Napoleon had no female heirs except possibly that child with Lady Beckett. So that's the route to take."

"The route to take?"

"Mitochondrial. And taking the sample from bone or teeth in the tomb."

"And in Brussels, swabbing the inside of the cheek?"

"Yes. See, the technicians will be dealing with Napoleon's DNA—if it *is* Napoleon and you use mitochondrial analysis. Then using the descendant's DNA as a reference sample and employing a concept called 'the most recent common ancestor through matrilineal descent', the lab can be the hero in all of this."

"Whoa! I said no fancy terms. But I get the idea, and you think we're going about this the right way?"

"Yes I do, but leave it up to Sylvie. She must be very familiar with the whole process. She's going with you?"

"I hope so."

Leon called a half-hour later. "All set for tomorrow," he said. "Two-thirty at 2004 Muller Street, just off the center of the city. The taxi driver will know. The woman's anxious to meet you and will be glad to answer questions, though she said she doesn't know what all the fuss is about. She's certain she's related to Napoleon. Seems like a nice person. Also she knows about your wanting a DNA sample."

"How did she react to that?"

"She'll cooperate but wanted to know why."

"And?"

"I kept it vague. I'm not even sure myself. But I said we have some new information about Napoleon and the sample might help determine how he died. And she dropped the subject. When you get there you can elaborate if you wish, but I don't think you'll have to. So to repeat the address, she's at 2004 Muller Street."

Paul wrote it down, his mind already on something else: There was still no indication that Leon suspected the tomb-opening idea. And Paul wasn't ready yet to broach the subject. He first wanted to discuss it with Maurice, but that would have to wait until tomorrow.

Paul was exhausted but before retiring he phoned Sylvie's apartment. She agreed to accompany him to Brussels on the condition there would be no talk about their relationship except as it applied to the mission.

Monday, May 29

The Thalys Bullet trip to Brussels took an hour and twenty-five minutes and the taxi ride to Sophie Bauer's apartment took another fifteen. Paul had reasoned that the fewer people conversing with the woman, the more comfortable she would be; hence he had convinced Vincent not to go along. Meanwhile Sylvie, from the moment she put a swab kit into Paul's briefcase, was more talkative and upbeat than usual. Paul had slept till nine and felt well rested for the first time in days.

Of his dozen textbooks over the past twenty years, the first was the initial installment of a series devoted to European history. It dealt with northwestern Europe. Paul considered Brussels one of the most important cities of that region for two reasons: one, its location—along with neighboring Antwerp, Bruges and Ghent—smack in the center of major trading partners France, The Netherlands, Germany and, across the North Sea, the United Kingdom. He wrote about the peculiarity, as he characterized it, of the country's sharp division into the Dutch-speaking *Flemings* to the north and the French-speaking *Walloons* to the south. Within Brussels itself, both French and Dutch are spoken.

The second reason and the one having greater impact on other major countries including the United States was the key role of Brussels in international politics and economics. It provided, and continues to provide, headquarters for both the North Atlantic Treaty Organization and the European Union.

Thus, while Paul had written extensively about Brussels, he had never been there; and now, if he hadn't been wrapped up in his "mission within a mission"—the DNA sample—he would have preferred to explore the city and its environs for a few days. He regretted having once written the ill-conceived sentence: "The smells and sounds of a bustling Brussels were not unlike those of New York City, only in miniature." He could still feel the sting of those historians from universities other than Yale who roundly criticized him for writing about some countries he hadn't observed first-hand. Eventually, in a guest editorial, he answered those critics by unleashing a salvo of his own: "Some academicians I know have written about hell, but have they ever visited it? Not yet anyway."

In any event, this was not the time to see the many historic sights of Brussels. The taxi left them off at a major intersection near a narrow alley which the driver pointed to as Muller Street. And in their short walk, they came upon no suspicious characters. No one stalked or tailed them; no one regarded them with murderous intent. Paul scrutinized them all as they passed by. He peeked into shop and restaurant windows, glanced at rooftops and even looked hard at a beggar to whom he gave an American five-spot. He still packed the Stealth 9 mm at his ankle, however, but since Sylvie had "come clean" he doubted there would be a need for it.

The weather had turned blue skies nippy since they had crossed into Belgium, and Paul wore the best of three suits he had packed for Paris, a dark pinstripe. Sylvie wore a cropped blue jacket over a white blouse and a print skirt.

It was 2:05 when they arrived at the small complex on Muller. Sophie Bauer ushered them into the living room of her second-floor apartment, an airy, colorful five- room space laid out in an L-shape. Paul and Sylvie bumped into each other as they maneuvered to determine who should lead the way.

"Don't be nervous," Sophie said in a husky voice. "You have a friend in this seventy-year-old. Anyone who might show me my true ancestors is welcome here." Smooth complexioned and cosmetic-free, she was short, trim and straight, all features that Paul would have attributed to a younger woman. She was dressed casually and colorfully: loose tangerine jersey, loose tangerine slacks, tangerine slippers.

They sat in a grouping of three easy chairs, each a different shade of soft red. Paul and Sylvie declined tea or coffee.

"You speak very fluent English, Ms. Bauer," Paul said.

"Please, I'm Sophie. Your kind formality brings me back to my students, first and second graders. They were all dear to me but I'm retired now."

There was an awkward gap in the conversation before Paul said, "You do know I'm sure, ah, Sophie, the difference between a European and an American?"

"There's a difference?"

"Yes, the European speaks more than one language."

All three chuckled, Paul uneasily.

He decided not to waste any more time. "Well," he said, "here we are, hoping to make history. I should begin, Sophie, by stating we're not about to identify your family tree scientifically. We're assuming that Napoleon is indeed your forebear. And that a certain Lady Beckett bore a child by him, a baby girl. Now when we get your DNA analyzed—Mr. Cassell mentioned that, didn't he?"

"Yes, he did."

"Well after that analysis, we'll work backwards to confirm or disprove your direct line to those two individuals. You've no doubt heard of Lady Ashley Beckett?"

"No doubt," Sophie answered. "The golden-haired beauty." She grew pale around the mouth.

Paul, momentarily taken aback, looked at Sylvie.

"She had golden hair?" she asked.

Something began to gnaw at Paul.

"Yes, definitely," Sophie responded.

"Why are you so certain?" Paul asked.

"Because my grandmother told me. She knew everything about the four or five generations before her."

Paul wasn't sure how to phrase what he had in mind, nor where he would take it once he started. "Did she ever say that each of the succeeding generations produced at least one female offspring?"

"All of them."

"No males?"

"Not a single one. I always thought that was unusual, but maybe not."

"And from your grandmother to the present?"

"Well, she had only a daughter—my mother. And my mother had two children, a girl and a boy. The girl was me, obviously. A year after I was born, my mother disappeared, leaving me to be raised by dear Ada, a distant cousin by marriage. I miss her. She told me my mother had another child sometime later. The boy, my brother. As for good old mom, I have no idea whatever became of her, and Ada, except for the child thing, never talked about her *or* my brother. I got the feeling she knew about their whereabouts but for reasons of her own, didn't want me to know. Maybe after all was said and done, it was the right thing. She was a bright and caring woman."

Sophie's voice had gotten huskier. Thick. Gravelly. "Would you excuse me for a minute?" she asked. "I'm going out to the kitchen for some water. May I bring you some?"

"No thank you," Paul said and Sylvie nodded. He saw Sophie take a tissue from her pocket as she left the room.

When she returned, Sophie said, "That must have been a verbal rat maze for you. Let's go back to Ashley and her golden hair. When it was described to me, I remember thinking of the English fairy tale, *Goldilocks and The Three Bears*. I used to read it to my students every year.

That's it! Golden locks! Paul reached onto his briefcase and fumbled through the samples of love letters before finding the one supposedly written to Lady Beckett. He ran his finger down to the line, "Your smile and golden locks fill my waking hours," read it aloud, then handed the letter to her.

"Have you ever seen this, Sophie?" he asked calmly.

She scanned it. "No," she replied.

"Could you please read it? And do take your time."

Sophie read the letter quickly and went back to reread specific sentences. "That's her all right. I mean it was meant for Ashley, without question."

"How about the English garden?" Paul asked.

"Sure. That's Beckett Gardens in London. They're still there I hear."

"Have you ever seen them?"

"No, never."

"Why not, may I ask? Or is it too personal?"

"Heh … this is *all* too personal, but that's okay." She swatted away some imaginary lint from her thigh. "I suppose I should be proud that I'm a descendant of Napoleon Bonaparte. Most days I am, but I'm also ashamed that my own blood may be unofficial. And, you know, it's one thing to learn that my grandmother's birth was unofficial. I can accept that. But to see where her golden-haired ancestor might be buried, I'd just as soon not go near there. One thing is what Hearsay? But the other is real. You can see it, touch it. It's oh so hard to explain my feelings." She looked at the ceiling pensively. "Let's just say I've stayed away from the gardens in case her grave is there."

They chatted briefly about things irrelevant from Paul's perspective. He nodded to Sylvie who then reassured Sophie that the procedure would be quick and painless. She deftly swabbed Sophie's inner cheek and smeared the swab onto a microscope slide. Next she allowed both the swab and slide to air-dry before packaging them and placing the package in Paul's briefcase. They stayed to chat for only a few more minutes. He asked for and received Sophie's phone number and stated that she would be kept apprised of any significant results. Sophie hailed modern science and wished them luck. Both Sylvie and Paul thanked and hugged her warmly before leaving.

As Paul inserted the key into his hotel door, Vincent ran toward him from a near corner of the hallway. He looked like one who had just spotted a long-lost brother.

"Am I glad you're back!" he exclaimed.

"Why? What's up?"

"The prior's been looking for you. Says it's important."

"Oh? How many times did he call?"

"Only the one time but I could read urgent in his voice. I almost tried to contact you and would have if he'd called a second time. Here's his number." He handed Paul a slip of paper.

Paul flung his briefcase onto a chair, but suddenly recalled that it contained the DNA sample. He hurried over to straighten and pat the briefcase as if it held a chunk of kryptonite. He then marched to the nightstand and sitting on the edge of his bed, put in the call to Frere Dominic.

"Paul? Good. Earlier today I received disturbing news that a group left London to seek you out there in Paris."

"Seek me out?"

"That's the expression he used."

"Who's 'he'?"

"Graham Radford. Our *histarian* there."

"Where did he get the information?"

"He has a whole bevy of informants."

Paul scrunched his lips. "What kind of group? Did he say?"

"He used the word 'unsavory.' When I asked him to explain, he said 'known mobsters.'"

"Here we go again," Paul said, cradling the phone in his shoulder and scratching his finger. "Sounds like a posse in reverse. How big a group?" He really didn't want to hear the answer.

"Four men. They left this morning. One of them had supposedly spent half his life in prison for shooting his girlfriend and for two attempted murders on the same day. Goes by the name 'Alec the Assassin.' Look, how far along are you in solving your … your conundrum?"

"Not far. A few more pieces have to fit into place."

"Well, may I suggest you have a bodyguard?"

"I have one. Vincent. He was with me when we came to the monastery, remember?"

"On second thought, could you arrange full police protection? I mean twenty-four-hour coverage. Leon could help with that, couldn't he?"

"Yeah, I'll ask him. I guess that's the thing to do. You know, Dom, I should be unhinged, but I'm beginning to get used to it and that's what worries me more than anything."

"I can understand and I'll do some praying, but what you just said is why you need help. Protective help. I don't think we should hope for dangers to blow away, and because you've got so many things bubbling up in your mind, you can get careless. Plus you're too close to everything. Let others worry about your safety."

Paul couldn't argue with the logic of this advice and responded, "Thanks, Dom. I'll follow through with Leon provided you follow through with something you just said."

"What's that?"

"Pray."

After hanging up, Paul told Vincent about what the prior had said.

"We have no choice, Paul. We're both armed but if they're hellbent on completing a job, only a heavy police presence will stop them. And I mean heavy. We'll need it anyway if we go ahead at the tomb."

Paul allowed himself to fall back hard on the bed. He ran both hands down his face and said, "Christ, I'm so tired of making phone calls here, making phone calls there. Interviewing here, interviewing there." He rocked back up and added, "But I admit we have no choice."

He placed a call to Leon whose number he now knew by heart. He gave the nature of the call and Leon didn't hesitate. Shortly he would, as he put it, deploy a counter patrol: two uniformed police officers keeping vigil in the lobby and two more stationed at Paul's door. All four would accompany or follow him wherever he went. Leon also agreed to a meeting in the hotel's coffee shop at two the following afternoon.

Paul stood abruptly and stretched his arms to the ceiling. "What say, Vincent? Time for dinner? I don't know about you but I'm famished." He stripped to the waist. "I also need a shower. You call Sylvie, fill her in and tell her to be here within the hour. Ten-to-one our police squad will also be here by then."

Chapter 30

Paul was right. Forty-five minutes later, just before 7, he answered a knock on the door but only after being satisfied through a series of questions and answers that a police contingent had done the knocking. He invited the four men in. Sylvie had already arrived dressed in black slacks and jean jacket over an azure blue top. Vincent hadn't gone home to change from clothes more wrinkled than matching: blue trousers, light green shirt and a faded maroon jacket. Paul stood awkwardly covered only by a towel secured around his mid-section.

Each officer eyed them from top to bottom and then one spoke up: "We've been asked by our good friend Leon Cassell to provide, shall we say, support for three important people, and I assume that means you. Which one would be Paul?"

Paul felt foolish raising his hand. "I am, officer, and I thank you for responding so fast. In case you're wondering, I just came out of the shower."

"Yes, it looks that way," the officer said. "Now rest assured that all of us are trained in this kind of duty. And on top of that, Leon and I had a good orientation talk about some possible danger you might encounter. Leave it to us, sir. We'll be quick to neutralize any threats that might come your way while you're in Paris. So go about your business and we'll handle any and all contingencies. We may not be in your line of vision every second, but you will be in ours."

"Well thanks again, officer. That's very reassuring," Paul said.

With that, the officers reeled around, soldier-like, and walked out.

Sylvie and Vincent gave broad smiles of satisfaction.

The trio had decided on *The Brasserie* for dinner, just down the street. Inside it was the simplest of restaurants, a single room with booths along three walls and a small bar and swinging door to the kitchen along the fourth. Spicy aromas and cigarette smoke hung in the air. At first, Paul disliked the loud echoing conversation they walked through to get to their seats because he thought they'd have to shout to be understood. It had always been a "thing" with him: a crowded room without carpeting and with paperless walls to absorb the "chitter-chatter." But on reconsideration, he concluded the noise would drown out their own talk as well.

Two of the police officers materialized out of nowhere and were seated nearby. They appeared to be kidding a waitress.

At their table Paul said, "Can we eat in peace and not talk about the mission for a change? For the next hour, let's screw the mission!" Vincent nodded. Sylvie thanked a different waitress who dropped off a basket of bread and butter, even though she had gone beyond earshot. Their silence lasted about two minutes.

"He's got to see it's the only sensible thing to do," Paul said.

Sylvie corrugated her forehead. "Who's got to see, and what sensible thing?" she asked.

"Leon. Opening the tomb. There's so much indication for it. Indisputable. I forgot who said what, but things like opportunity to steal the body, substitute a double. Imposters are nothing new to Napoleon. Yeah, sure, imposters when he was in his power days—security reasons—but when he's near the end? Why? Then we have all the loose ends. The amended codicil. Where the hell is it? Beckett Gardens. Should we check it out? Lady Beckett's golden hair. It's in the love letter. Sophie referred to it too. These point to something significant but I'm not sure why. Is it because ancient DNA, with a few mutations thrown in, can't prove beyond a reasonable doubt all by itself, and the golden locks can't do it by itself either? But taken together, they can prove the body is Napoleon's? If that's who's lying at Invalides in the first place. So Beckett had golden locks. Big deal. But then again, it shows that she was Sophie's great-great-great- whatever. And we have Sophie's DNA. I don't know. I really don't know. One minute I think I understand it and the next, I don't. One thing I'd swear to though: we've gone as far as we can go, short of opening that tomb."

Sylvie and Vincent had let him ramble while taking it upon themselves to order a bottle of red wine for the three of them. Paul hadn't noticed the waitress with pad and pencil.

"You know what?" he said. "I'm talking in circles. Let's just eat."

The following morning at precisely 9:30, Maurice hobbled into the coffee shop to join Paul who, a minute before, had winked at the police officers as he passed by them and then claimed one of two unoccupied tables. Maurice greeted Paul by doffing his black beret. Settling into a chair opposite him seemed to be a major undertaking for the Frenchman, who rested his cane on the chair between them. Paul detected no alcoholic smell this time.

"Glad you called, Paul. Maybe you'll bring me up to date. I mean from your point of view. Leon does a pretty good job, but I like to hear important things right from the horse's mouth."

Paul gave a synopsis of the events at Elba and St. Helena but concentrated on the visit to Brussels. He detailed the value of DNA in identifying ancestors and the necessity of opening the tomb to obtain a sample. Before he had a chance to mention Sophie's comment about Lady Beckett's golden hair and how it squared with Napoleon's love letter, Maurice spoke up.

"I'm in favor of that, Paul. Going right to the tomb itself. Yes, I am. The man was poisoned, no doubt about it, but why would that mean there's an imposter in his tomb? Did they ever think back in 1840 that someone would have the audacity to check his burial site sometime in the future? And if they did, did that mean they had to cover up and substitute someone else? Would arsenic stay in his bones all this time? Did they think it would last forever? It can, come to think of it. But that's not the point. The point is who's in there and how did he die? I mean Napoleon. I don't give a hoot about any impersonator. But is going in there to get a reliable sample of his hair worthwhile? All those hair samples that have suddenly surfaced—who's to say they're really his? Go right to the source, I say. See if it's Napoleon, then do whatever the scientists say to do to see how he died. Take a fresh look. And if it's not him, then we have to ask why not, and that I can't answer as we speak."

Paul wondered how it all would have sounded if he *had* smelled alcohol on Maurice's breath. "You make some good points," Paul said. "So welcome to those of us who vote to open the tomb. It's unanimous thus far."

"What does the young whippersnapper have to say?"

"Vincent? All for it." Paul believed Maurice had asked the question only to get another dig in. "The one I'm concerned about though, Maurice, is the president of *Vérité* himself."

"Leon? He'd be a fool to object, and he's no fool."

They both ordered rye toast and coffee.

"Once he's on board and he will be, he'll arrange everything because he's got more connections than a power plant. And rest assured, I'll pitch in. I think there should be a military presence, not only for added security but also as a fitting symbol of what Napoleon represented for so long. Also some crack soldiers should be stationed nearby just in case, and I can see to that."

"In case of what?"

"In case of anything."

Chapter 31

Paul sat at the same table in the same shop. It was after two. He untied and retied his shoelace. The only difference from the morning was that the cigarette smoke odor had turned visible.

In the morning he had wanted to obtain not only Maurice's input but also his backing before he spoke to Leon. A matter of more ammunition, of shoring up support. And though he was prepared, his mind grew foggy as Leon lumbered in ten minutes late. Suddenly Paul felt the giant was a stranger who needed convincing about jumping over the Grand Canyon.

"Sorry, Paul. Traffic snarl," Leon said, squeezing into a chair, cigarette dangling from his lips. Paul had never seen him wear a sweater before, jet black and vertically ribbed in design, unsuccessful in conveying an impression of slimness.

"Thanks for coming," Paul said, "and I'll get right to the point. You asked me about two weeks ago to undertake a monumental task. I did and I've spent more hours on this case than I have in locating stolen diamonds in Zaire, artifacts in Morocco and paintings in Germany—all combined." It was a line he'd planned on using.

"And you've accumulated vast amounts of information."

"Yes, I have."

"And that information has led you to a *sine qua non* in your investigation."

"You might put it that way."

"So you want to open Napoleon's tomb."

Paul shot upright in his chair, his face feeling glazed with shock. "But …"

"So do I", Leon said. "There never was a question, to my way of thinking, that it would come to that. And I knew all along that you were thinking the same thing. Don't ever get serious about the game of poker, by the way."

Paul summoned whatever adrenaline hadn't been siphoned off into the emotion of the moment. "I, ah, that's about the sum and substance of what I wanted to talk about. And you knew all along. May I call you a rascal?"

"Yes, I knew all along. And yes, you can call me a rascal if you'll permit me to use an old expression that I believe originated in your country: 'What d'ya think I am? An empty suit?'"

Their laughs were lusty, genuine. And, in Paul's case, filled with relief.

Leon went on. "But, yes, it's got to be done, and with Maurice's help, we can arrange it. The sooner the better. We'll get the proper permissions from our government and from any other group they counsel us about. We'll use personnel from the *Prefecture de Police* including the proper equipment and workers experienced with blowtorches. We'll bring in military personnel if Maurice thinks it's necessary. We could consult with cemetery people and the like but I'd rather stick with the police and the military. They can keep a confidence. They're used to it. We'll shut down the area, you know, for repairs. Rope it off, canvass it off from floor to ceiling, keep visitors away."

"Can it be done in one day?"

"I believe that's plenty of time."

"A lot of unsoldering and unsealing. Six coffins in all, one inside the other."

"Yes, I know, but it shouldn't be a problem."

Paul liked the pace of their conversation. It screamed speed. He tasted it.

"When can we go ahead?"

"How about tomorrow? Early. Say, seven? That'll give us three hours before the tourists stream in. Meanwhile, I'll get workers to shroud the area tonight after seven, closing time."

"You can set it up that quickly?"

"Why not. A call here, a call there."

"What if you meet some resistance?"

"Believe me, it doesn't matter. If I do, I proceed a different way." Paul sensed the big man wanted to elaborate and he was right. "Someday," Leon said, "I'll explain, but for now let's just say I have all kinds of chits out there and if I can't call one in for whatever reason, I call in another."

"So the bottom line is that you'll have everyone ready to go at 7 in the morning and all I do is show up?"

"You got it, with one exception. Don't minimize your role. We'll see to it that Officer DuBois will direct the operation. I'll be there too, but in the background. He'll be instructed to answer to you, not me."

They shook hands. Leon walked out and Paul sat there, pondering. The police officers at the opposite end of the coffee shop saluted him and he saluted in return. He noticed they were munching on biscuits.

Paul started for his room but decided to step outside for a dose of healthy air. He felt energized, for never in his wildest dreams could he have imagined the meeting with Leon would be a cakewalk. *So much worry for nothing.*

Outside he waved to the other two officers who were sitting in a police cruiser diagonally across the street. As he took a long deep breath his head lifted and he casually looked up. The top floor of the five-story office building straight ahead was lined with windows, all closed shut save for one at the far left end. He tried to avoid the glare from reflections off the glass, all the while guessing that the single window was cracked open about a foot, at most two. At first it didn't register as anything important and he even thought little of a linear flash of light coming at him from that single crack but upon shielding his eyes, he confronted the light head-on and observed it changing shape—to a smaller, sharper ball of fire. *A rifle! The shiny steel barrel! Then the muzzle!*

Paul darted behind a car parked at the curb in front of him, turned around and pressed backward against it and waited to allow his breathing to slow down. The specter of his body rolling into the gutter tore through his mind. Then he pushed himself off and raced into the hotel, shifting his weight from side to side like a football halfback zigzagging through tacklers.

Once in the lobby, the outside officers approached him from behind. "What happened?" one of them asked. "You looked like you were staggering."

"Just a little dizzy spell. I get them now and then. Tension."

"And you're sweating."

"It's a hot day." For a moment, Paul thought about describing what he had seen but dismissed the idea out of hand. He was too focused on the morning ahead, as menacing as the incident was. And he even decided he would withhold mention of it to anyone else, fearing it might somehow jeopardize the plans for Invalides.

Paul had visited the Church of the Dome and Napoleon's tomb twice before but had never imagined he'd one day be involved in taking the tomb apart. He, Sylvie and Vincent arrived at the marble gallery overlooking the sarcophagus at 6:55 a.m. Leon had led them through a slit in the massive canvas curtain outside the gallery. Sylvie carried a Styrofoam container, presumably to secure a bone fragment taken for DNA profiling.

They were introduced to Leon's wife, a small woman by comparison. And to Officer DuBois, some government officials and several historians attached to the Hotel des Invalides. Maurice was there. Two members of the clergy were there. A woman with a videorecorder was there. Off to one side, twelve uniformed policemen stood at attention as did six medal-laden military officers on the other side. In the crypt below, ten workers in white jumpsuits and black caps circled the tomb, their eyes trained on DuBois like a starter in a road race waiting for the signal. He in turn stared at Leon. Two of the workers wore headlight sets similar to those used by coal miners, although the lighting was more than sufficient. Two ladders leaned against the elevated tomb. Metal scaffolding was in place on two sides. Various tools lay on a wooden platform an arm's length from them: hammers, circular saws, wedges, crowbars, chisels, screwdrivers, blowtorches. Conversation was sparse and hushed.

Paul remembered his last visit when he had stood almost in the same spot gathering material for his latest Napoleon book. Clipboard in hand back then, he was making notes and sketches of what he was observing and of what he had previously read. And now, he took out a card containing notes he'd used for the final draft of that book. He read:

At crypt level, the sarcophagus, consisting of a casket within and a scrolled cover, and made of red porphyry, a variety of granite, rising high toward the double cupola and pendentives of the dome. The elaborate bronze door leading to the tomb is flanked by two colossal bronze figures that bear symbols of imperial power on a cushion: the crown, the sword, the globe and the hand of justice.

At gallery level, the six chapels around the gallery but currently outside the canvas recently installed.

At the base of the sarcophagus, a multicolored, star-shaped mosaic recalling Napoleon's eight most famous triumphs: Rivoli, the Pyramids, Marengo, Austerlitz, Iena, Friedland, Wagram, and Moskowa. And circling around, twelve winged statues in Carrara marble, symbolizing victory.

Paul, at the time, and again now, imagined the emperor enclosed in six coffins placed one inside the other. He knew their composition by heart: the first of tin-sheeted iron, the second of mahogany, the third and fourth of lead, the fifth of ebony and the sixth of oak.

What followed was a series of nods. Leon nodded imperceptibly in Paul's direction. Paul's nod was more obvious. "Proceed," Leon said to DuBois who nodded to the workers below. The dismantling began.

The men worked swiftly and in harmony. They freed the tomb off its support structure and lifted it onto the scaffolding. Their grunting pierced the dead silence. They managed to move the tomb to ground level. Later, when they reached the final coffin, Paul felt unsteady as he slid sideways for a better viewing angle. Sylvie took hold of his hand. He believed the answer to the question was moments away. *Please let it be Napoleon and not an imposter.*

Four of the workers lifted off the lid and gasped in unison.

Paul turned marble white. “There’s no one there!”

Chapter 32

After recovering from the shock, Paul and the delegation huddled at the rear of one of the empty chapels. Leon deferred to Paul who, despite the somberness of the occasion and their meeting place, barked out requests and instructions.

"If my hunch is correct," he said, "a little visit to London will go a long way in wrapping this up.

"Where in London?" Sylvie asked. "Beckett Gardens?"

"You got it." Paul answered. "You'll come?"

"Absolutely."

"And bring that DNA container?"

"Yes, of course."

"And you, Leon, you can contact the *histarian* there? Radford is it? We need to notify whoever's in charge of the gardens to expect us. Give us permission to look around. Snoop, if necessary. I'll take care of any request to dig after we get there."

"Yes, Radford. Very efficient. He'll set the scene."

Paul excused himself, said he'd be right back and broke away. He walked out the door, through the slit in the canvass and, hardly noticing the workers collecting their tools, fixated one last time on the empty coffin, as if to verify what he had seen only minutes before. Or what he had *not* seen. He ran a finger slowly over his lower lip, wheeled and walked back into the chapel. For the first time, he felt as challenged—obsessed—with locating

Napoleon's body as he was in determining the manner of death. The corollary, he reasoned, was that the body itself might offer major clues as to whether he had died naturally or was murdered.

The Beckett estate, once an expansive tract of floral land with mansion, riding stable and assorted outbuildings had been deeded to Edenshire Township in the early 1900's as part of a nasty and well-publicized foreclosure. The mansion and other structures were gone now, the entire tract having been converted into a cemetery abutting London's northern edge. The designation "Beckett" was retained, however, and the area variously identified as "Beckett Cemetery and Gardens" or "The Cemetery at Beckett Gardens" or simply "Beckett Gardens."

Lady Ashley Beckett had been the mansion's most famous occupant. "Famous" as in "infamous", for to some she was an outcast; to her family members a disgrace. Her prodigious appetite for amorous alliances was never a secret and even a possible affair with Napoleon Bonaparte had been mentioned as a seduction on *her* part.

Nonetheless, upon her death, her heirs buried her there on the land she treasured and erected a massive headstone rivaling that of Henry Fielding's in Lisbon. Its inscription read:

Lady Ashley Beckett
Entrepreneur and Friend to Many
1795-1845
May She Rest In Peace

At 4:00 p.m., Ansel, Leon's personal pilot, landed the light plane on an Edenshire airstrip not unlike the one in Paris. Paul, Sylvie and Vincent were aboard. Through *histarian* Graham Radford, Leon had arranged for a supervisor and three-man digging crew to accompany the trio to the gardens for an "inspection." The supervisor had raised questions about such a designation but was silenced and rewarded in no uncertain monetary terms.

The cobblestone entry drive to the gardens was bordered on both sides by stone pots on rock pedestals, pachysandra, rose geraniums, towering sycamores and plain trees. Far off in the distance were row upon row of gravestones in a sea of the yellows and reds and blues of early flowers that Paul couldn't identify. Fifty yards in, the supervisor pointed to Lady Beckett's headstone, off to the right. And it was there that Paul stated he wanted to begin their inspection. He urged the inspector to leave after assuring him that no defiling would take place, no damage done. The diggers, he said, would be used only to move away some earth in one or two areas suspected of housing old unmarked graves overgrown with vines, sod or mixed vegetation.

Paul stood studying the area, then moved to a spot directly behind the headstone. In its shadow, the growth appeared thin, a fact other observers might have attributed to shielding of the sun by the ten-foot high marble slab. *But they're not looking for shallow headstones!*

Paul dug an inch into the ground with his foot. Two inches. More as the dirt seemed less compact. Then he met solid resistance.

"Here," he said to the diggers. "Could you please dig around here?"

They complied and within the length of a shovel blade, there was a clang. Paul had never conceived of trying to differentiate between the clang of metal on rock and the clang of metal on cement. But if he were now to place a wager, he would pick cement.

He felt the blotches come, asked the men to broaden the hole, grabbed a shovel excitedly from one of them and outlined a three-by-six-foot rectangular area around it. Before they had completely dug out the space, Paul looked at Sylvie and Vincent and shouted, "Pay dirt! Excuse the pun,"

He kneeled down and cleaned off a one-foot square cement block with his hand. It bore an inscription in tiny letters:

WAIT FOR ME, MY BELOVED
IT WILL NOT BE LONG
1840

Paul's words came quickly now as did his movements, almost twitchy.

"The coffin there," he said, "can you—would you—open it? Your boss would give the go-ahead, I swear to it. I'll explain to him later."

The bulkiest of the diggers started in and the other two followed suit. They used tarnished tools taken from a tarnished toolbox. It didn't take long: iron screws dangled from the coffin's rim.

Paul's, Sylvie's and Vincent's eyes stopped blinking as they beheld a mummified corpse before them. There were dirty cloth fragments over most of the wasted body, yellowed ornaments, medals and two swords. And at its feet, a small tin box, blackened as if it had lain in soot.

The corpse's skull had disarticulated from the rest of the body and lay at an awkward angle to the chest, the bones of which were riddled with pockmarks.

Silently the three of them put on surgical gloves. Paul picked up the skull and was about to hand it to Sylvie when he stopped short.

“What’s this?” he screamed.

He inserted his thumb into a circular hole in its right temporal side and the little finger of his other hand into a smaller hole on the opposite side of the skull.

“He was shot!” Sylvie shrieked. “That’s an entry wound on the right.”

Paul’s hands shook as he handed the skull to Vincent who had signaled he wanted to examine it. Paul then opened the tin box and withdrew two sheets of rag paper, stiff and brittle with irregular edges. Each contained a message written in the scrawl that, from having studied official French documents, Paul recognized as the emperor’s.

The first:

Amendment to Codicil
1st May, 1821

I ask forgiveness for using a terrible chemical that will over time end my life.

The second:

4th May, 1821

I write this alone without benefit of counsel and without foreknowledge that it shall ever be read, nor do I intend it to be, for it is only an instrument to purge myself of the decision I have made. If it were not for my dear Ashley this would not have come to pass this way, nor did the coercion delay fulfillment of my last wish. I requested her to supply the weapon that may or may not be herein included. She would not, or more properly, could not discharge it, leaving it for me to complete the task with my own hand. It was not a hasty decision on my part, arrived at only after an unsuccessful trial with the terrible chemical whose name I cannot bear to write. My guilt has no boundary and I leave it to others to decide if the ache is greater over my military defeats, my temptation in the face of the chemical, or my final act the result of which has now been witnessed. I await your coming, dearest Ashley. Long live my beloved France and its people!

Paul decided not to wait. He took out his cell phone and called Leon to pass on the news.

The reaction of *Vérité's* president was more evident in his voice than in his words: breathless, loud, raspier then usual. "I can't believe it," he said.

And Paul's voice was just as breathless as he tried to cover as much as possible before they met again. "But there it is, Leon. Napoleon's manner of death was neither criminal nor natural. *It was suicide.* An awful sight. An awful-looking casket, falling apart, the body deteriorated. Can we meet in the hotel lobby at about 7:30? I'll give you my theory of the background. For now I'll just say the body was stolen in 1840 when it was supposed to be transferred to Paris. No doubt Lady Beckett was behind it. I see Talleyrand's hand in it too. She wanted Napoleon buried in her gardens and expected to join him there later. Now we have to prove it's definitely his body. The writing looks like his, I must say. The DNA business will take a few weeks in a case like this. Eventually I'll work up a written report for you."

"Forget the written report. You've kept the delegation well informed. I know I speak for them when I say you've convinced us beyond a reasonable doubt. It's what they want in a court of law and we can't ask any more than that. Excellent work! You grew on the job, you know. We all saw it."

"Thank you, ah, sir. Speaking of the delegation, you'll inform Maurice of what we found?"

"I certainly will. And Paul?"

"Yeah?"

"Thank you so much for changing history."

PART FIVE

Chapter 33

After personnel at the Hollings Questions Division welcomed Rick back, he was handed several questions to consider taking on. But the idea of even reading new questions and handling one himself had pretty much lost its appeal. He leveled with the four administrative assistants and they offered no comment.

"It's like that sunrise out there," Rick said, pointing at a window. "Perceive one, perceive them all. They keep coming and we keep noticing; and for the most part, we keep enjoying. But what happens when a storm is brewing? Do we sulk? Do we tear up? Of course not. The same with the questions and me. What I've faced is like an honest-to-goodness storm, but I'm not tearing up."

Yet one of the men handed Rick a question and said, "I understand but look at this."

Rick did so and his mouth parted slightly but no words came out until his brows raised and then lowered.

"Hmm" he said, and did a complete about-face. "Maybe you should forget about my complaining; this looks interesting and would require little or no traveling because I've already written about all of it over and over again.

The inquiry was phrased:

> Is Nazi plunder still around? Looting of Jewish assets like gold, paintings, books, religious, treasures. If so, what can

> be done to stop it or minimize it? And where does Vichy France fit in?

Rick was suddenly consumed with intertwined intrigue and finality as he realigned his thoughts.

> The last one … do you hear? The last one!
>
> Then limit all energies to security issues at Hollings General.

As to the question, he believed that the best part of it dealt with not having to travel to verify the answer. For example, he'd written about Nazi plunder so much, and amassed articles and newspaper clippings about it all, that any travel for its sake, would only lead to redundant information. And the same applied to the status of Dracula. To a degree or in a different way however.

In any event, although he had put "Dracula" high on the list, he would postpone its consideration for the time being.

He decided to label the summary of issues that needed consideration as a "Gang" and to arrange for its *contents to be* stopped or minimized. It included:

1—Nazi plunder, as mentioned.

2—The status of Dracula, as mentioned.

3—Hospital receipts being diverted to money laundering, kickbacks, cybercrime and other organized criminal activities.

4—Stopping Swiss banks from accepting looted assets. Tightening the whole process.

5—How his whereabouts always seemed to be known

6—Vichy France.

First in the "Gang"was the newspaper article about Nazi plunder. He had skimmed through it originally, before storing it away in his satchel. He found it and read it more carefully, skipping no words:

During World War II, European Jews were victimized twice. Not only were they victims of the Holocaust, but they were also the victims of Nazi officials who stole from them. Homes were invaded and stores plundered. The trains came in to Auschwitz, a concentration camp in Poland, and as the people stepped off the train, not only were they separated from their families, but they were ordered to place their belongings into baskets — clothes in one, books in another, jewelry in another, gold in another. Everything was separated. From wedding rings to gold fillings from teeth, the Jews' possessions were then melted into gold and sent to Switzerland where Germany acquired hard currency to carry on the war effort. As the Nazis swept across Europe, they confiscated gold from each country they invaded. The money contained in Swiss bank accounts from both of the central banks in Europe and Holocaust victims is said to be in the billions of dollars. As the Nazis shipped valuables to Switzerland, they made extensive use of the safe deposit boxes there. American documents have been related that there are hundreds of millions of dollars in bank vaults, composed of jewelry, securities, artwork assets, and valuables. So of it was returned — most were not.

While doing so, he was perplexed about something: repeating the same story in his writings. But after reading about this one, he sat down and spent time ruminating until he came to a conclusion:

It's bound to happen when a prolific author writes one book after another; and another; and another.

In fact, it *had* happened in his previous book — *On the Right Track*. The same stories involved the Holocaust and Lucky Lindy.

Dracula was next on the list and, as stated, Rick would defer to another time — after he had conferred with (1) Fabio Calderone, and (2) Victor Frelinghuyens, close friend of the Mafia.

Third involved hospital receipts. Have Joe Gomez arrange for his international crime buster friends to handle it.

Fourth was the Swiss banking problem. The solution here is multifaceted: (A) Names of depositors to be advertised. (B) Threaten imprisonment for certain bankers — those who accept such deposits and those who say they're thinking of leaving the country. (C) New suspicious deposits to be stopped. (D) Seek Vatican help. In return for Swiss Guards defending the Vatican and acting as papal bodyguards in Rome, knowledge of Swiss banking practices had never been revealed. Now they should. As a side issue: roughly 50% of the Swiss population is Roman Catholic.

Fifth involved Rick's whereabouts. To be investigated. In fact, he sometimes wondered about his whereabouts in the first place!

And sixth was the Vichy France history. Some background about a Vichy France and Swiss connection is relevant here. It's been well known that the Nazis forcefully collected Jewish assets and hid them in Switzerland banks. But there were other facets to the connection.

In June of 1940, the German army occupied Paris and Henri-Philippe Petain became France's new premier. He worked very closely with Adolph Hitler. In effect, they divided the whole country into occupied and unoccupied zones. The Germans controlled three-fifths of the country. The rest was left for Petain to administer. And it became known as Vichy France. It really amounted to a puppet state of the country. One aspect of this scenario was that all Jews living in any part of France had to surrender to the Germans. This meant that Petain had to help round up as many Jews as possible with all of them headed for concentration camps and eventual extermination. There was even some talk about Hitler and his German associates wanting to create a master race that would comprise the whole world.

When Rick felt he had devoted more than enough time to the question, he wrote out an answer to be given to the four hospital associates. And taken as a whole, it wrapped up that phase of his life. Almost.

For there had never been a time when he hadn't taken stock of his immediate past, and so often it had lost its immediacy and blended in with bygone but related experiences. Here, there were the travels, the characters, the threats and challenges.

Epilogue

1--Regarding Rick's whereabouts, Transylvania's Alex Prisco was arrested based on his being seen snooping around the Chandler house on a regular basis. Even around Hollings Hospital. He was always taking notes while seated in a black Dacia station wagon.

2—Money laundering, kickbacks, cybercrime and other organized criminal activities were not eliminated but were diminished when hospital receipts were better monitored.

3—Fabio Calderone and Victor Frelinghuyens arranged for **bad** Mafia figures to kill the Dracula imposter.

4—Rick hadn't expected hospital security responsibilities to be as burdensome as they turned out to be. But he enjoyed it.

5—He decided to stop lecturing during the foreseeable future.

6—With Fabio's assistance, he continued his friendship with **good** Mafia figures.

7—He and Angela began traveling while paying little attention to sightseeing. Their goal was to pass through all of Connecticut's 169 cities, large and small.

(for reference only in Draft form)

Test Contents

www.ingramcontent.com/pod-product-compliance
Lightning Source LLC
Chambersburg PA
CBHW030817310726
48980CB00006B/532/J

* 9 7 8 1 9 2 8 7 8 2 7 1 1 *